AVEKE

AN AVA AND ZEKE NOVELLA

TIJAN

To all those who began rooting for Ava over the Fallen Crest and Crew series.
For those who hated Zeke, then began to love him.
Or those who just loved him right away.

NOTE TO THE READER

Ava and Zeke are characters both introduced within the Fallen Crest/Crew/Rich Prick world. I've written their book so it could be read as a standalone, but within that world, it is the newest and latest addition.

For more information, you can go here.

1

AVA

He was here. Again.

This was, what? The fourth time this week. Eight sharp. The last four evenings in a row. And he came in, took the stool at the far end, and sat. Just sat. His head bowed. He took a breath before he lifted his head, and he paused, like he'd needed one second before readying to slip on the mask that the rest of the world saw. Then he tipped his head back, his eyes went to the television right above him, and as Brandon gave him a beer for the night, he'd sip and watch his best bud play soccer on the TV. And like tonight, if it weren't his best friend's team playing, we'd switch it to another game. Score if it was someone we knew playing, because around these parts, that wasn't that uncommon. But not tonight.

There was a hockey game, but not the team he liked to watch.

Brandon wasn't working tonight since I had told him twenty minutes ago that I'd close for him. Brandon had a woman, and he was happy, so he was starting to let me close most nights for him. So tonight, I moved down the bar, meeting Zeke's eyes briefly before he saw me reach for a tall glass and pour his favorite beer from the tap.

He was tired. I caught the wariness before he switched. A wall came over him, and then he reanimated to the cocky jerk that most people took Zeke Allen for being. Wealthy. Preppy. If that was still a descriptor for someone our age. We're in our twenties, so I suppose instead of preppy, we could use the word 'blessed' to describe him. He didn't seem like he aged.

Muscular. Big broad shoulders. He had the physique of a bodybuilder. Dark blond hair.

A very big square jawline, but it was so prominent, that it alone could get so many women in bed with him. I'd seen him in action many a night, and he never had to work hard. He tended to buy them a drink, ask them how they were, and within a few minutes (always depending on how long Allen wanted to chat), they'd head out.

Zeke was gorgeous when we were in high school, not that he and I attended the same school. With our neighboring towns, one could say I was on one side of the tracks and he was on the other. The privileged. He went to a private school, which seemed to get more private and exclusive as the years passed, and I was from Roussou. It used to be a good place, alive and thriving, and then it took a turn and not many seemed as privileged there anymore. I think it was doing better these last few years due to some local businesses that brought in a bunch of people, but still...it was hurting.

I finished his pour and took the remote for the television. Placing both before him, I gave him a nod. "Think Kansas City Mustangs are playing tonight."

He grunted, took a sip, and picked up the remote. "Thanks, Ava. Thinking I'd like to watch the Javalina tonight."

He was already changing the channel before I turned to fill another order.

I knew Zeke would sip his beer and want another in twenty

minutes. Then a third on the hour. He'd stay almost to closing, stopping long before he'd need to drive to sober up. Once a guy with the reputation for being a bully and an obnoxious jackass, he wasn't like that anymore.

Eyeing him from the corner of my eye, I wanted to ask what happened to change his ways. One day.

2

AVA

"Ava, why are you single?"

We were on beer number four of the night. He was on this round a little after one in the morning. We closed at two, but if Zeke needed extra time, I wouldn't kick him out. He could stay while I closed up. I had no problem with that.

I grunted, sliding his beer over to him. We were on the late-night sports highlights, and the place was going strong. It didn't bother me. I was the only one behind the bar, but I had a system down.

I grinned. "Why? You volunteering?"

He grinned back, a chuckle before lifting his beer. "Just seems weird. You were with that Roy guy for a while, and then..." His eyes grew distant, and his head cocked to the side. He was thinking, trying to remember my love life, but he wouldn't remember because while he went to a D1 school, I stayed home and attended the local community college. There'd been plans for more, to finish and go on to graduate school, but life got in the way.

I knocked my knuckles on the counter in front of him. "Don't think too hard, Allen. I'm single because I want to be." I moved down the counter. Three women had been eyeing him all night, and they were on their fourth round of shots. The one who'd been paying all night waved more money toward me, so I started reaching for three more shot glasses.

"No. Wait." She leaned over, and I got a good whiff of her perfume mixed with booze as she breathed on me. "We want a shot with him too. Four shots."

I didn't move, but I looked at Zeke from the corner of my eye.

This had happened before. Many times, and Zeke was always a good sport about it, but for some reason, I was hesitating. That wasn't good for business or my job, so I grabbed the Patron. "You want them poured here or by him?"

She hesitated too, and I saw some self-consciousness set in. Her two other friends were ignoring us, almost gawking at Zeke. She bit down on her lip and leaned over again. "You know him?"

I nodded.

"What do you think?"

I opened my mouth but faltered on what I was going to say because the truth was, Zeke would've already grabbed one of them if he was interested. The girls were not being subtle, and he knew the game. He was a master at playing it.

"How about I pour yours here and take his to him? He can wave you down to say thanks?"

Her smile was wide and quick. "That sounds great!"

I did as I said and ignored the other two girls' grumbling as I took the shot to Zeke. I placed it a little away from him and bent down, pretending like I needed to grab something under the counter. "Giving you a heads-up. That shot there is for you, paid for by those three girls. Yellow halters." (Every single one was wearing yellow.) "And they're hoping you'll wave them down to thank them for the shot."

He barely reacted, taking the shot, flashing them a smile in thanks, and he tipped his head back for the shot. He mouthed it, then followed with his water, and as he set that glass down, I saw that it grew a little bit more water than what had been in there.

I looked up, caught him watching me, and he gave me a wink.

My pulse jumped, and I almost dropped my washcloth because fuck, my stomach got some tingles.

I looked down, surprised. I hadn't had this reaction to someone in a long time.

"You're Zeke Allen, right?" One of the girls came over.

His gaze stayed on me for a moment before turning to her. "I am." He gave her a once-over before smirking. "Please tell me I didn't fuck your older sister or your mother."

She gasped.

There was the old Zeke I remembered. I'd missed the jackass.

He slid off his stool and threw a bunch of bills onto the counter. Ignoring the girl, he lifted his chin up toward me. "You're too hot to be single, Ava. That's what I think." He knocked his knuckles on the counter before heading out.

"What a dick!" The one girl was scowling in his direction. Her two friends joined, and the second one (not the one who paid for all the drinks; she had stayed back the whole time) huffed at me, her hand finding her hip. "You don't have to laugh at Laughlin. I thought we were in the whole women empowering and lifting each other up era?"

I fought against rolling my eyes. "Sweetie, I wasn't laughing at your girl. I was laughing at Allen, because for him, *that* was tame." I began moving backward, going back down the bar. "Also, Laughlin is a cool name."

The girl eased up, her head straightening. "Thank you."

A guy had moved in behind the girl who paid for everything, and as I filled his order, I couldn't help myself. I asked under my breath to her, "They're going to pay you back for tonight?"

She jerked upright, stiffening. "I don't know what you're talking about."

I stepped back, eyeing her. "Right." I gave her a soft, but sad smile. "Here's some female empowering two cents: if you gotta pay for them, they're friends with your cash, not you."

She flicked her eyes up, just as the others called her name. "Whatever." She stalked off.

I watched her go, but I didn't know why.

Maybe I saw a bit of me in her. Sadly, it wasn't the part that had friends. It was the part that felt like a schmuck. That was me back then, and still was.

I lied to Zeke. I wasn't single because I wanted to be.

I was single because no one that I wanted, wanted me back.

3

AVA

The house was lit up when I got home, but that wasn't uncommon.

I walked through, turning off everything. Grandmum's oxygen machine was buzzing in the background, but I still went in and made sure everything was working properly. She was settled in her bed, folded up like a ball, and turned to the side. She was so tiny, but that was a family trait. All the women were petite. All of us had blond hair too. Grandmum's was white by now. Mom's was dark blond, and I was a mix between with honey-light blond hair. I saw a tip of Grandmum's hair sticking outside of the blanket, but otherwise she was fully covered. I stood in the doorway, watching out of habit to make sure her chest rose. Once I saw the steady rhythm of her deep sleep, I turned her light off too.

It was her habit to leave it on. She once told me she kept it on because she never knew when Grandpap was coming home, and the habit had stuck. She couldn't sleep unless the light was on. Growing older, learning more, I was figuring she kept it on in case he tried to sneak in after they separated. He never gave her a divorce. That was one thing he held over her head, and how my grandmum grew up, she didn't fight him. She was just happy he never brought his shotgun to finish her off.

Women shouldn't have to live like that, but some did. Grandmum did.

I left her room and checked on my mom next.

She'd taken to the same habit as Grandmum. Her light was on, and she was sleeping in almost the same position as her mama. The main difference, her wheelchair was positioned next to her bed, and she didn't have an oxygen machine. Instead, though, she had a fan propped up for noise.

I turned her light off and moved through the living room. That light too.

Doors were locked. I checked them two more times before I headed upstairs.

None of the lights were on up here, but neither my mom nor Grandmum came up here. It was the reason it was mine. I got the whole floor, but I only used the large bedroom on the end.

I cleaned up and got ready for bed.

Once I settled in, my window was open because temps were fine at night, I rolled to my side. I faced the door and the one window I had propped open. That was it. I couldn't handle sleeping with noise. If someone broke in, it was up to me to protect everyone. That was my role in the family.

I took a deep breath, feeling sleep starting to spread through me, but right before I drifted off, I flashed back to Zeke.

"You're too hot to be single, Ava. That's what I think."

I drifted off with a grin on my face.

I didn't believe him, but it felt nice to hear.

4

AVA

The smell of bacon and coffee woke me, and my stomach grumbled, waking me even further.

I knew my mom could cook just fine. She was a wizard in her wheelchair, but I still hurried getting up for the day. I didn't shower last night because I didn't want to wake anyone up. Both needed their sleep, so I hurried with a shower this morning.

I grabbed my phone, pulling it from the charger and stuffing it into my back pocket before I went downstairs.

The sounds of the grease sizzling filled the room, along with the coffee machine brewing.

I was already smiling before I got to the kitchen because my mom didn't need to cook for me. She and Grandmum liked to sleep in. Not me. Or I didn't think I did. I never had, to be honest. Sleep was a privilege for me because I worked so much, so her doing this was for me.

They also weren't big breakfast eaters, though Grandmum would nibble on some dates when she woke.

But once I hit the doorway, I saw the brochure laid out on the table and my heart sank.

This wasn't going to be one of those happy mornings.

I looked over.

My mom was watching me. Metal tongs clutched in her hand, she'd unlocked her wheelchair so she could see me better.

Tiny, but toned arms. Her hair was clipped back with tiny barrettes, framing her face from ear to ear. They were rainbow colored. She had on mesh shorts.

She swallowed, her eyes flaring from grief before she said what I never wanted to hear from her.

"We need to talk about Grandmum."

5

ZEKE

We were on the golf course when instead of lining up his shot, my buddy burst out laughing.

I frowned. "Dude."

He was almost falling over, but turned to me, raising his nine iron behind him. "Zeke! That is fucking hilarious. Look!"

Brian was almost falling over from his laughter.

Jesus. What the fuck.

I got out of the golf cart and moved so I could see whatever this was. When I got there, holy...*fuck*. But I wasn't laughing. Ava was walking across the green, but not in a way where it was obvious that she was on a mission or had a destination in mind. No. She was going this way, then that way, and going in a circle. She was walking backward. She was all over the place, and she was drinking from a bottle of vodka at the same time.

I drew in a breath as Brian kept laughing. "You know who that is? That's that Ava chick. You know, the one who worked everywhere." His laughter went up a notch. "We'd go to the pizzeria. Ava. We'd go to Manny's. Ava. We'd go to Nooma's. Ava. It became a joke, remember? We'd drink if she popped up somewhere. She was at the gas station too. Damn. Girl got around."

One day I'd tell Brian how close he was to getting his face punched. Or how close he was to waking up in a hospital bed. I didn't trust myself right now.

He sighed, his laughter finally fucking subsiding. "I doubt she works here. She's as wasted as I was on my twenty-first birthday."

"Brian." Finally, I could speak, through gritted teeth.

"Yeah?" He swung my way.

"*Shut the* fuck *up.*"

"Wha—she's not in our social circle. What are you doing?"

Ignoring him, I started down the hill, carrying my own alcohol in hand.

"Zeke!"

I raised a middle finger in the air and yelled over my shoulder, "Take care of my shit."

"What are you doing?"

I raised my middle finger higher.

By the time I got to her, he was gone with the cart.

Ava had no idea I was there. Her head was down except when she'd tip it back for a drink, and she was moving in a way —I saw the headphones. She was dancing, listening to whatever as I saw her pull her phone out of her pocket and skip to the next song.

It was a lively one because she began jumping around, her head going the opposite direction. Her arms were doing...something.

I wouldn't call this dancing. It was more like flailing around with a baseline of rhythm.

I watched her for two complete songs before her eyes opened. Seeing me, she startled, gasping, and a screech came out of her at the same time.

I smiled and held up a hand. I mouthed, "Hi."

"What?! I can't hear you!"

I nodded, pointing to her headphones.

Understanding dawned, and she started laughing, pulling off the headphones. "Hi. Sorry. I forgot I had them on." Her music was blaring out of them. She didn't move to stop or pause the song. She was frowning at me, half-squinting. "Zeke? What are you doing here?"

I cocked my head to the side. The glaze was minimal. She wasn't slurring. She was speaking like she was sober, and without the electrocuted dancing, she now looked sober too.

I was somewhat impressed.

"Right." I motioned around us. "We're on a golf course, where I do the normal douchey thing and golf a few times a week, and your question is as if I'm the one out of place."

At my words, she jerked her head around, sweeping in the entirety of the Fallen Crest golf course. Her eyes were almost bulging when she focused back on me. She spoke in a shocked whisper. "What am I doing here?"

I was nodding, but I edged closer and reached out, taking away the vodka from her hand. She didn't notice. Then I almost started laughing. She'd barely drunk any. Maybe two shots' worth. "Are you drunk or not? I'm having a hard time telling."

"I think I'm drunk."

"You barely touched this."

Her gaze snapped to the bottle as I raised it, and she looked confused. Her eyebrows came together before she held her hands up, both of them, and gasped. "I didn't even feel you take that."

She *was* drunk.

She raised her gaze back to me, her hands still up in the air. "I parked at Manny's, grabbed a bottle, and just started walking. I wasn't paying attention. Dancing, drinking." Her voice dropped low again. "I've never drunk before."

Whoa.

My head went back an inch. "Never?"

Her eyes still wide, she shook her head at the same time. "Never. I accidentally went to a party once because my boyfriend was the local Uber. He went to pick someone up and I had to go to the bathroom. He thought I went in to stay and join the party."

I... I had no words. I was quite aware that most of my life, if there was a night I didn't party, *that* was the oddity.

"Oh my God. You're looking at me like I'm a freak." Her face flooded with color, and she closed her eyes. She was still holding her hands up.

"Okay." I didn't know what was going on here, but I moved in, took both her hands, and lowered them for her. She opened her eyes, and there was no reaction that she knew I did that. "Have you eaten today?"

She shook her head.

"You want to eat?"

"Um." She started chewing on her bottom lip, her eyebrows still pulled together. Then she stopped. Her face cleared. She blinked. "No. I need to keep drinking." She grabbed my beer and took a long draw. I was waiting for the sputtering, thinking she didn't realize she reached for the wrong bottle, but nothing came. She kept drinking.

I got fixated on how her throat was working, chugging that down.

She was taking long and slow pulls, and she kept going.

It clicked she just chugged a third of my beer and I had a thirty-two ouncer with me today before I grabbed it back. "Stop."

She reached for it, stepping with my arm.

I moved, turning and using my body to check her. "No."

"But—"

I raised the beer so she could see it clearly. "That wasn't yours."

Her mouth opened. She was going to argue, but she stopped. A gasping sound came next before she slumped, her forehead falling to my arm. It was raised right in front of her. She moaned. "Oh, no. I'm so sorry. I'm a mess."

If two shots of vodka already had her wasted, that beer was going to finish her off.

I glanced back to the country club, but she'd be a mess there. I didn't think Ava would want people seeing her like this.

Taking her arm, I began to walk to the parking lot.

"Wha—where are we going?"

"You need some food."

She started to put on the brakes.

Nope. I wasn't having this.

And I wasn't questioning myself why I was doing any of this as I let her go, put both caps on the alcohol, and stuffed them into my pockets. I had large pockets. Then I turned, bent down, and picked her up. She was slung over my shoulders.

"Wha— Zeke! Put me down!"

I kept going. "You need food, Ava, or you are going to regret that beer. Trust me."

Being slung over my shoulder probably wasn't the best idea, but I didn't want to waste time fighting with her.

She tried to raise herself up, so maybe she was thinking the same thing. "How do you know?"

"Huh?"

"How do you know I need food?"

Right. She never drank before.

"Of the two of us, I'm thinking we should go with my knowledge of drinking."

"Oh." She got quiet. "That's a good idea."

Food it was.

6

AVA

This was what being drunk felt like. Huh.

I was sitting in Zeke's kitchen, in a chair, by the table, in the corner, in his kitchen—I already said that— and whoa. Wowee. I moved my head upside down, or as much as I could, and the kitchen looked amazing this way too. We should all look at the world this way.

Wait.

I twisted around, laying my head down with my feet up, and oh yeah. This was so much better.

We could walk on the ceilings. The shelves could be benches. It made so much sense now.

"What the fuck are you doing?"

"Huh?" I swung my head around and WHOA! Zeke was like a god. Standing. Defying gravity. Staring down at me.

This was amazing.

I was having a spiritual event.

"You're going to get sick if you don't sit upright."

I started to tell him that would defeat the whole point, but I felt a rush of nausea coming on and he *was* a god. He totally knew what was going to happen before it happened.

Then I let go and fell. I crumpled to the floor, and oomph.
That hurt.

Hands touched under my arm, and I was being lifted. I
moved, not thinking, just reacting, and when I blinked, I was
clinging to Zeke like a monkey. Legs around his waist. Arms
around his shoulders and he was holding me in place with a
hand under my ass.

I almost wiggled because that felt kinda good.

I'd not done anything with a guy in so long. It was embarrassing. Made me feel pathetic at times, but then I remembered
why, and oh yeah. That was real-world shit. I didn't want to deal
with real-world shit.

"Hey." Zeke's voice was all soft. He was watching me, his
head angled back so he could see me better, and the concern in
his gaze was undoing me. He frowned a little. "Why were you
drinking today, Ava?"

I didn't want to look in those eyes anymore.

I turned, my throat closing up. I blinked away a few tears,
but dammit. One got free, sliding down my face.

Zeke walked us over to a counter. He shifted, putting me
there, but he didn't move back. Reaching up, he cupped the
side of my face with such tenderness.

Still undoing. A second tear got out.

He wiped both away with his thumb, but he was still
holding my face. "Talk to me. I've known you for a long time,
but I've never seen you like this."

He was right. I worked. I was strong.

I never broke, ever.

Not when my grandfather was finally arrested and we were
safe.

Not when my father left us.

Not when my mom lost her legs.

But today—I was losing everything.

"My grandmum is going on hospice."

I felt Zeke tense, and I closed my eyes, waiting for him to pull away.

I didn't really know Zeke. It was a weird budship that started with us because he was just as lonely as me. He, who had the world at his feet. He could go anywhere in Fallen Crest and people wanted to talk to him, be seen with him, but he'd begun changing.

I knew he was fierce about some of his friends, one of his best friends, but that best friend was in Europe. Was that it? He was missing that friend?

"You changed when your best friend came to town."

He stiffened again, but a surprised chuckle left him. "What? Topic change there."

I relaxed a little. This felt safer to talk about. "You both were gods at your school. I watched. I saw everything. You were such an asshole, but then Blaise came to town and a different side of you came out." I was back to whispering, confessing, "I liked seeing that, though you terrified me."

"I did?"

He didn't sound surprised.

I nodded. "You were a bully, Zeke."

He frowned, his body still tense, but now going rigid. "I know." His tone was rueful. "That changed, but I never should've been what I was."

"Was it your best friend who changed you? What happened?"

His eyebrows went up, and he was almost talking to himself. "Man. I... Yeah. Blaise coming back helped because he stood up to me, put me in my place, and I was a jackass. I needed that, but it was other stuff too." He laughed a little. "My dad caught me taking something I shouldn't have, and well, he kicked my ass. Not physically, but he took everything away. Like house staff, my car, money. Everything. I had to take care of the house. It was normal what he did, gave me structure. I needed it. He humbled me a lot, but I realized he actually loved me. Like real love, where he gave a fuck if I was growing up to be a future white-collar criminal or not."

"Really?"

He nodded. "Nothing super traumatizing or anything. I just got some love that was missing. My dad stepped up. Blaise was back in my life. And I made a conscious choice to look for good guys to be like. I didn't want to be lazy. I wanted to be a better person and yeah. Fast-forward a few years and I guess here I am." He grew more focused. "What about you?"

I tensed. "What do you mean?"

"What happened to you? You were always quiet, hardworking, but you weren't jaded. I saw you too."

Flutters moved through my belly. He had?

I thought about all the hard times, and I shook my head. There was no beginning and the end... I couldn't go there. "Life. That's all."

"Life?"

I nodded. Pain sliced me, and I felt a knife being shoved into my throat. "My mom told me today that when Grandmum goes into hospice, she's going with her. She's going into a facility, said it was time."

"What about Grandmum?"

"It's time, Aves. We had a talk, and she wants to do a hospice bed in the nursing home. There's a room there they can use for her."

"When did you decide all of this?"

"I had a meeting with them today."

"No. No, Mom. We can take care of her here. I'll get time off—"

"Ave." She wheeled her chair closer and stopped, folding her hands in her lap. *"You have taken care of us most of your life, and honey, you're too young for this. I'm going to move into my own place."*

"What?!"

"*It's not that bad. It's a new program. It's set up where I'll have my own place, and I've got some friends there already.*"

"*You're not old. What are you thinking?*"

"*I'm thinking we need to sell the house to handle some of the extra bills, and I'm thinking that I want you to live life where you're not taking care of me anymore. You can help, but it's not like I'm dying anytime soon. It's not what it sounds like. It's my own place, but I got people close to help if I need it. I don't want you to worry about me.*"

"*You're my mother. That's my job. That's not going to stop if you move somewhere else.*"

"*See. Right there. That's why I need to make this move. You know I've got some other health concerns. They ain't going away.*"

Grandmum was dying. My mom was moving. We needed to sell the house.

I was losing everything I knew.

7

ZEKE

Jesus. I was stunned.

Ava told me what was going on, and pieces were fitting together as to why she worked so much. How she must've felt in high school, and I had been such the opposite that I was getting another humbling kick in the ass. Right up the ass.

Fuck.

I couldn't comprehend any of this.

"You're amazing."

Ava gave me a weird look. We'd moved to the living room. The conversation continued as I brought in a pizza, and she was looking tired. I was thinking some of the carbs were soaking up the alcohol. She wouldn't be so sick, but she was also feeling what she'd been hoping to avoid.

"What?" She laughed, but I saw the confusion too.

I leaned forward, scooting to the edge of my couch. "You're amazing, Ava."

She quieted, her eyes widening, and she seemed to slink into the loveseat, like she wanted to disappear.

I shook my head. "I was such a jackass in high school." I leaned back, my eyes still on her. "My mom's an alcoholic."

"I didn't know that." She said that so quietly. Small.

I snorted. "It's not a big deal, at least to me. To each their own, I figure. She thinks it's her getting by, but she's just wallowing. She doesn't want to change. Alcoholic or not, she's a good mom to me. She just likes her wine, and then she goes in her room and cries. Or she did. Her and my dad are on some big trip so I'm not sure if it's the same deal, but that's how I grew up." Thinking on it, I winced. "I mean, I don't like that she's that sad, but that's for her to fix. Anyways, sharing that because I've always known I didn't need to take care of my parents. And I've always known that there'd be assets for me. I never worried about any of that, and you, I don't know the breakdown of health insurance or whatever and you've not talked about the males in your life or even if there were or are any, but you're fucking amazing, Ava. You're looking at me like you've got no clue why I'm saying that to you, and that makes you even more amazing."

All the sex. The booze. The literal stupid shit we did in high school. The drugs. Then college. Joining a fraternity.

And she was here. Working. Caring for her mom, her grandmother.

I'd been living life, but I'd not been appreciating it while I did it, and her, she hadn't been living, but she would've appreciated every second of it if she had.

Fuck.

Fuck!

She was there, here, under my nose, and I never saw her.

"Why'd that jackass let you go?"

"Jackass?" She was back to whispering.

"Your boyfriend in high school. Didn't you have another one? Earlier too?"

"Oh." She shrugged. "Roy. Just grew apart. He's got a new fiancée now."

"He's a dumb shit jackass then." I shook my head, only

looking at her now. "And the other one? He was a worse jackass, wasn't he?"

She shrugged again. "He was a learning phase, that's all. That's when things were starting to go bad for my parents, my dad, and I clung to a different type of guy. He turned out to not be good for me, but I got out of that relationship. Roy was the opposite of him, and what I needed at the time."

"Want me to beat him up?"

Her lips twitched, the faintest smile, and damn, that sight made my heart race. "No. That's okay."

I grunted. "You sure?"

Her smile grew, and that was a reward by itself.

8

AVA

Time went too fast and too slow all at the same time.

After that day with Zeke, we packed up Grandmum and moved her to the nursing home. I worked full-time at Manny's, but I also worked part-time at a horse stable outside of Fallen Crest. It was new, and the main point was to offer boarding and equine therapy. It had recently become a place for rescue horses as well. I liked the balance between the two jobs. One was pouring drinks or serving people food, and the other was helping with the horses. I did most of the office work, but there were times I snuck out to the barn and spent time with the horses. There was a magical calmness to them that was addictive once I picked up how to feel it. I was in good standing with both jobs, so they let me scale back time in order to be with Grandmum.

My mom and a few of her friends were packing up the house, and she took me to her new place.

She was right, as much as I hated to admit it. It was a one-floor apartment in a house, and it was all hers. The whole place was wheelchair-accessible, and I met some of the housemates on the other floors. Next to the building was a health clinic, so they had nurses there and they had a system if any assistance was needed for off-hours.

It was a good setup for her.

And I was at the grocery store, because she needed food since she insisted I take most of what we had.

"Ava?" I was in aisle eight, grabbing soup when someone said my name.

I frowned. "Jarrod?"

"Hey. Hi." My ex before the last ex, the jackass I'd been just talking to Zeke about. Had our conversation brought him back to town? He held a hand up, giving me a grin. He was taller, if that was possible. Maybe six-three. A faded jean jacket over a black muscle shit. Jeans that matched his jacket, frayed, worn, but also trendy. His dark hair was messy. He was super tan, but not in a great way, though judging from the smirk he was giving me, I was thinking maybe he didn't agree with my last thought.

Jarrod always thought he was the king shit. I was thinking that hadn't changed. He was as lean as he'd been back in high school, but he seemed more solid.

"How are you?" He moved closer, holding a bag of bread in his hand. Nothing else. He motioned around the grocery store. "I saw you when I was grabbing my stuff, and thought there was no way it was the same Ava from back in the day. But it is. Look at you. You look great."

He had hit me. On more than one occasion.

He had torn me down, one insult after another.

When I was happy, he wanted to take that away, and he had. Every time until I learned it was better not to be happy around him.

All those memories came flashing back, pushing to the forefront, and behind them was the reason why I was here in the first place. To get food for my mom, because she was moving, because it was time to sell the house, because my grandmum was dying. Other decisions that had happened without my say, that were affecting me, just like he had.

"What are you doing here?"

He gave a shrug. "Family reunion. We're camped out at Kade Campsite. You know where that place is? It's new, but pretty cool."

"You're only in town for the reunion? You're leaving right after?"

His eyes sparked, and not in a nice way. He began to open his mouth, but then–"Ava, you were getting the soup? I was supposed to get the pizzas." Another person joined our group, and Zeke stopped next to me, looking down at his phone before lifting his face. A frown in place, but Zeke made sure to step somewhat in front of me before seeing Jarrod. "Oh, hey! You're Jarrod Oster, aren't you?" He held out his hand. "Zeke Allen. You remember me? We went to different schools, but I remember you."

Zeke and I hadn't talked since that day he helped me when I was drunk. It was a bittersweet moment for me. The first time I got drunk. A friend helped me out, and we talked the entire rest of the day. He made food for me, showed me his beautiful home before he gave me a ride home and then saw where I lived.

I was proud of our house. It wasn't much. A bit run-down with peeling paint, a few cracks in the sidewalk, a few rotting porch posts, but it was my home. It would always be my home. Of that, I was very sure. Everything else, not so much, but I'd never have another home like that.

So yeah, when Zeke dropped me off, a part of me could've shriveled up in embarrassment.

That was the younger me. This different me stood proud and I brought him in, showed him around, and we sat and talked even longer in my living room.

I must've fallen asleep because when I woke up, I was in my room and he was gone.

That'd been six days ago.

Jarrod had gone still now, his head edging back before he straightened to his fullest height. "Yeah, man. Allen. I remember you, too. Academy, right?"

"Right." Zeke's tone was dropping the friendliness, and he edged even more in front of me. "You left school back then. Why the fuck you back?"

Okay. Yeah. All pretenses were gone. Zeke's tone was low and dangerous, a warning.

Jarrod's head snapped back, but those eyes turned mean too. "I'm saying hello to an ex-girl–"

"She's not your ex." Zeke was fully in front of me, his back to tight and tense, though his tone was almost soft. Eerily. "She's not your anything because the time you had back then wasn't anything, but haunts and lessons. Lessons like never going for another guy like you again. You taught her that." His head clipped down in a nod. "Now, you get going. I'll pay for your bread if that's the case why you're still standing here, being all hesitant."

"You might want to watch–"

"No," Zeke shot out. "I don't think so because unlike Ava, I know where you've been. And I know another guy who was in the same place. Potomahmen. He's all the way connected too. Won't be too much work to give him a call if I need to."

Zeke was talking about a prison nearby.

I edged to the side and saw Jarrod narrowing his eyes at Zeke. "You're lying. You don't–"

"Call my bluff. Please."

Zeke wasn't sounding bothered or ruffled. He was speaking cool and calm, and that was giving me shivers down my spine because I could feel how he *wanted* Jarrod to call his bluff. This was a glimpse of the old Zeke, back from high school. He was still in there.

"I don't think so, man." Slowly, almost achingly slow, Jarrod reached out and put the bread on top of a bunch of soup cans. "There's another store I can go to." He began to pass us by, but stopped, his head low. "You might want to not see me around town, but I got a feeling I'll be seeing you. If you know what that means."

"Yes, dumbass. It's your witty way of trying to threaten me, but you see, you're just not smart because now I *gotta* make that phone call."

Jarrod sucked in his breath, but took off, stalking away. I felt singed as his gaze swept over me.

Zeke circled around, watching him go, before I could feel the instant he was out of our aisle. A whole weight lifted up off my shoulders. I frowned at Zeke. "Why did you do that? What were you talking about, making a phone call?"

He was still facing the aisle, but his eyes cut sideways to me. "I got curious about what you said about him. I did some digging on the internet, that's all. And he knows who I'm talking about with the phone call. He crossed paths with someone that Blaise's brother knew, who's connected to some dangerous people. That's all."

My whole body went cold. "I'm not liking this, any of this. I don't want you to make that call."

He moved so his body was facing me. He gave a small nod. "Okay, but I'll handle him another way."

"What way?"

He shook his head, a small grin toying at the corner of his lips. "Maybe better if you don't know, but he'll leave you alone. I do promise that."

I wasn't sure what Zeke could promise, but he seemed so certain so I was going with trusting him. He had connections of his own, and Jarrod had taken off quickly enough. The old

Jarrod would've been duking it out in the grocery aisle within two sentences. Either he had matured since school or Zeke's reputation stood for itself.

I was going with Zeke's rep, but I did ask, "Potomahmen? Was he really there?"

Zeke was still tense, but drew his shoulders up, held, before lowering and as they did, a softening came over his face. "Yeah. According to his own social media, he was."

I glanced down, saw his hands were empty. "What are you shopping for?"

"I'm not." He leaned in and took the list that I'd bunched up in my hand. "But I am now. I saw you pull in and also saw him following you."

"What?" Another shiver trickled down my back.

Zeke looked up from the list. "He saw you drive in, and purposely followed you. I saw him and followed him. He wasn't in here shopping for food. I'm betting he was going somewhere else, saw you, and thought to try his hand at making a meet again." He studied me as he spoke. "He's not good news, Ava. His social media alone shows that, but was I wrong to step in? Did you want to rekindle something with him?"

"No! My God, no. I'm just not used to someone doing all that you did."

He snorted, bumping his shoulder into mine lightly. "Don't know why you aren't. You're hot, Ava. Already told you that." He grabbed for some of the soup that I had on the list and put them in my basket, at the same time as he took the basket out of my hands.

I grinned. "Is that the only reason? 'Cause of my looks?"

He shot me a grin in return, and it rocked me back on my feet. It was so light, but dirty, rakish at the same time. I had no idea how he managed all of those together. He said, "Might have something to do with how you're like a saint. Kind. Loving. Got your shit together." He had started further down, grabbing some canned vegetables next, but then stopped and looked right at me. "Or maybe it's because you're one of the good ones. You're the one that any guy would line up for a shot with, even just for one chance, and that guy will regret it for the rest of his life if he lost that shot. Your ex? He's regretting."

He said it so seriously, piercing me, that I felt a whole different zing go through me. One of shock, but also wariness. Zeke wasn't fucking around. He was going straight to the heart of the matter.

He shifted closer, lowering his voice. "You know that, don't you?"

My throat was swelling up, and I had a feeling that Zeke wasn't going to let this drop so I jerked a nod. And I lied. "Totally."

His eyes narrowed. His head cocked to the side, and he lifted up, tucking a strand of hair behind my ear before trailing his finger to just under my chin. He lifted it up, just slightly, before his hand fell away. "You will one day."

9

AVA

I was just arriving to Manny's, the first night in a long time that I'd left Grandmum's bed.

I had to.

I didn't *want* to go, and I wasn't scheduled, but I couldn't stay there. I couldn't sit there, watching her go, knowing my mom was leaving too (in her way) and it got too much for me. Work was my escape. It was my constant. In a way, work was my home, and once I stepped inside Manny's, I felt like a part of me could breathe.

I didn't know how to "just be." I needed movement. I needed busy.

I needed chaos.

I needed Manny's.

As soon as I stepped inside, Brandon was frowning at me. He gave a nod to Derek, our other bartender, before slipping away and heading toward me. "Your grandma?"

I shook my head. "I need to work. I'm not scheduled, but do you need the help? I just... I need to not think right now."

He was studying me and frowning at the same time, but

then a kind smile came next. "I'll always need your help. Any night of the week, any time. I hope you know that."

I choked up, my throat swelling, but I shoved that down and nodded. "Thank you." I moved past him, stowed my purse under the bar in the locked drawer, and after that, it was work mode only.

I FELT his presence before I saw *him*, and I only needed to look up once Zeke slid onto his stool.

His eyes were on me, narrowed a little. "Hey."

"Hey." I poured his usual drink.

"How are things?" The way he said it, it could've been casual, but I was starting to know Zeke. He wasn't intending it as polite small talk. He wanted to know.

"No Jarrod, if that's what you're asking about." I started to move away.

He stopped me, putting his hand over mine on the counter. "He's gone. He left town."

I left my hand where it was, with his on top. "Should I ask how you know that?"

His hand twitched, but a mask came over his face. "The internet's not that hard anymore. You can find almost anything on it."

Was that it? Just the usual cyberstalking? But he was doing it for me, on my behalf, and it'd been the second time he helped me out. I was remembering back to when I'd been at his house, when he'd fed me, when he took me to mine. When he was gone the next morning and how the next time I spoke to him was at a grocery store and he helped me yet again.

I didn't know what he wanted right now, if he even wanted anything.

"I know." I turned my hand around and started to link our fingers. "Maybe we can talk about it later?"

Just then, a presence interrupted us. A female slid onto the stool next to Zeke's and she did it with zest. It was an abrupt and almost coarse sensation, cutting into our moment. "Talk about what later?"

I stepped back, physically and emotionally pulling away. My hand felt like it'd been burned. I tucked it behind me.

Kit Carlson. She went to school with Zeke. She was in his social group, and she was watching me as she was taking off her jacket with narrowed eyes.

"What's going on?" She indicated me with a slight head nod. "Ava, right?"

I nodded. I didn't speak. That'd always been my role back in the day, and I was easily stepping back into it. Kit came around, but not that often. After college, she remained local, but I knew she married some big CEO-type of guy. I wasn't surprised.

She frowned. "Zeke?"

He was half-turned away, but at her last question, his shoulders drew up, and as they fell, the old Zeke shield was back in place.

He looked back, a half-smirk/half-grin was in place. His eyes lit up, looking mischievous but also dark at the same time, and he nudged her shoulder with his. "Nothing, Carlson. Or am I supposed to be calling you Hughes now?"

She snorted, easing back, and the narrowed eyes relaxed. "You can save that name for a different kind of hang out." Her smile was sly and seductive, and my stomach turned over.

They were sleeping together.

Or they had.

And she was married.

"What would you like to drink?" My voice came out clipped. Zeke stilled.

She didn't. She threw her hair back and extended her hand,

her nails freshly manicured and sparkling pink. "A rosé, and don't let the glass get empty."

Right. It would be one of those nights.

I poured her drink and remained at the opposite end of the bar for the rest of the night, giving Derek her instructions. I felt Zeke's gaze on me, but I heard her laugh, so I knew she was loving Derek's attention. He was a flirt. Wealthy socialites like her were his forte.

I tried not to focus on them, her with Zeke. I did. I really tried, but a few times I glimpsed over and saw how her hand was on Zeke's arm, or his leg, or how their shoulders were touching each other. She rested her head on his arm at one point, half-draped all over him.

My stomach kept churning until I couldn't handle it anymore, and why I was so pissed—I didn't know.

Whatever.

Zeke always slept around. He'd had a shitty reputation back then, and why would that change now? Even if he'd been kind to me a few times?

Who was I really? Nothing.

I stayed till closing, though Brandon told me I could leave. I didn't.

Derek went home. Brandon headed out. I insisted on doing the cleanup.

I had no clue when Zeke left or if he went with Kit. I went into the back, and they were gone by the time I came back out, but now, when it was almost three because I'd been dawdling, I heard a toilet flush in the back.

The door opened.

Footsteps sounded. Someone was coming down the hallway.

A shiver went down my spine. I thought everyone was gone, and I moved back, I'd already turned the lights off, and flattened myself against the wall. I could dart out the side door and run if I needed, but then the figure showed, and I released my breath.

It was Zeke.

"I thought you left."

He made his way to me, through and around the tables with their chairs turned upside down. His head cocked to the side. "I was hiding."

A snort left me, one that was a little too relieved if I was being honest with myself. I leaned back against the wall, content to let him keep making his way to me. "Hiding from who?"

He stopped just in front of me, and I could see his eyes from the parking lot light shining through the window. They were clear and very focused on me. He was sober. "You know who I was hiding from."

Kit.

"You and she are none of my business."

He took a step closer, still watching me. So intense. "Maybe I want us to be, maybe for one night?"

My stomach knotted up again. What was he doing?

I swallowed tightly. "I don't know why you'd say that—"

"I don't fuck married women."

My eyes closed. He went right there, straight to the point. I opened them again. "Did you used to?"

"I used to fuck Kit, yes, but not since she was married. I can be called a lot of things, but I'm not a cheater and I'm not disloyal. I like Kit's husband."

"She's a cheater."

"Again. That's not me."

"Are you going to tell her husband she cheats?"

Gah. Why was I involving myself? All my life, I was "less than." I was the working class. I never had money, probably never would. I'll work till I die, but until a week ago, I thought I'd always have my family beside me. I knew different now.

I was breaking. Right now. Right here.

I was looking at something I wanted, even if it was just for a night? Could I?

Did I dare?

I wanted to, so badly.

Zeke sidled closer, his eyes almost glittering from how fierce they were looking at me. "Kit and her husband have an agreement. They both know what they're getting out of their arrangement."

My mouth dried up. "Are those the sort of agreements you like?"

"No." Even closer. I could almost feel him. A slight twitch of an arm and we'd be touching. He added, "Again, a lot of words can be used to describe me, but I'm loyal. Once I care about someone, I lock on and I don't let that person go. It's a fault of mine."

What were we both doing here?

My head was spinning. I was confused.

"How's your grandmother? I didn't ask at the store."

Those words undid me. All the fight left me, almost fleeing in its retreat, and I folded. I began to slump down, but Zeke caught me. He moved in, his arms holding me upright, and his leg pushed against mine.

"She's dying."

"I know. I'm sorry. I should ask, how are *you* doing?"

I shook my head, a tear sliding down my face. "I'm here when I should be there. What does that tell you?"

He took a deep breath and moved in more fully.

His arms went around me and he stood there, holding me. It took me a second to realize he was hugging me.

A sob broke free, and I reached for him, grabbing onto his jacket. "Why are you being kind to me?"

He angled his head back, searching my face. A new softness came over him and he shifted so he could run a hand over my cheek, wiping my tear away. "Because whether you like it or not, I'm locked on."

That undid me all over again, and I reached for him, just needing him.

I was giving in.

I leaned forward, and my lips touched his. A soft graze because did I really want to do this? But it felt so good. *He* felt so good.

I groaned, a carnal need exploding in me, and I had to have more.

Had to.

I needed it like air.

He reached up, cradling my face as he pulled his head back, searching me. He saw something there that made him groan, and his mouth was on mine. He wasn't soft. He was hard, and I wanted that.

Mouth to mouth. I tried to devour him as he was trying to devour me.

Pleasure coursed through my body, filling me up.

I was scrambling, trying to push up his body because I was blind to anything but him.

An ache was deep inside of me as we kissed.

His tongue slid inside, claiming me. I let him. I was claiming him back.

God. Please.

This. So much of this. More.

Ignoring his jacket and shirt, I reached for his jeans and undid the button.

He stilled, his mouth leaving mine, but his head bent next to mine, and I felt his breath on my neck.

I kept working, undoing his zipper and I reached inside, finding him already hard and straining against my touch.

He groaned as I wrapped my hand around him and began stroking him. "Fuck, that feels good."

I was beyond words. My head rested on his shoulder as I kept working him. He held me until he stifled a curse, and then he batted my hand away.

I cried out, protesting.

He shifted again, this time he yanked my jeans and pulled them down, stepping on them to push them the rest of the way. Once they were clear, I was being lifted higher for him.

My legs wound around him.

Then he was there, his cock at my entrance, and he surged inside.

We both paused at the feel.

I moaned as he cursed under his breath. "Goddammit." His hand flexed, one cupping my ass and the other bracing us against the wall. "I can't go gentle. I can't—tell me that's okay. Jesus, Ava. Tell me that's okay."

"It's okay." I gasped just as he began to move inside me.

He went hard, surging in, sliding out, and sheathing himself right back inside of me.

Fuck.

It was intense. There was nothing smooth about this sex, but I loved it. Wave after wave of pleasure was crashing down on me.

He held me up, and I wrapped my legs tighter around his waist as he pounded me.

I saw stars when I came.

10

AVA

The next morning, my phone rang and it was *the* call.

Come to the nursing home because Grandmum was going. I rolled over in Zeke's bed, dressed, and didn't say a word. When I came out of the bathroom, he was dressed as well and waiting for me.

He drove me to the nursing home.

I went into the room and sat, holding Grandmum's hand and my mom's. I had no idea how long we sat there, but it felt like time stopped. A vacuum settled around us. It was only us, only what we were going through, and that was all that mattered. The other world kept going, but I ceased paying attention to it.

Me. Mom. Grandmum.

Until Grandmum left.

Zeke drove me places. He brought me food. He was in the background, always there.

My mom noticed him, but she never asked, and he never made a fuss to be introduced.

Grandmum already had everything planned ahead of time, so the funeral was small. A few neighbors came. Some of my mom's friends. But Grandmum had kept to herself. She had no siblings, and my mom didn't either, like me.

Zeke didn't go to the funeral. He asked if I wanted him there, but I didn't. I just wanted it small. I wanted to hold my mom's hand the whole time, so that's what I did.

It was a week after that when Mom's move was final.

A month later when the house was sold.

I had people who checked on me. My bosses from Manny's. My bosses from the horse stable. My colleagues from both places. Roy even called. There were still others, some people who thought kindly of me from high school. Two of my community college classmates. Flowers and food were sent, but now I was in my apartment and it was my first night.

My first night being alone.

I couldn't handle it.

11

ZEKE

Ava: Wanna come over?

"Dude." Blaise sat down in the chair next to me, spying my phone. "Who's that? You got a new girl?"

I shot him a grin but responded to Ava first.

Me: What's up?

I was very aware of my best friend watching me while I was waiting for her response. He didn't get back that often. His schedule playing for one of Hungary's football clubs didn't give him a lot of time in the off-season. But he was here, and I got to hang out with him, so we were making the most of it. A night at the house, drinking, playing FIFA, and planning on doing whatever. I loved my boy. Any time spent with him was good for my bro-soul.

But this was Ava.

Ava: Nothing. It's cool. I'll see you at Manny's later.

I frowned because Ava didn't call or text. She didn't ask me to come over.

Pushing up from the chair, I hit dial on my phone and went into the other room.

Her dial tone sounded before it went to voicemail.

"It's Zeke. Tell me what's going on. Call me back."

"Holy shit." Blaise stood in the doorway to the living room, his thirty-two ouncer in hand. "I have never heard you talk to anyone like that, with that tone of voice. Who the fuck are you and what have you done to my best friend?"

I shot him a grin, but I knew it was distracted, and I hit redial.

It went straight to voicemail.

Something was wrong. I felt it in my gut.

"Can you do me a favor?"

Blaise took a step backward. "Now I'm even more alarmed. You look concerned, and I swear, the last time I saw this look on your face was when you thought I was going to do something to land both of us in prison."

I grunted.

My best friend was smart and had hawk-like observation. He'd already deduced someone on the phone was important to me, and he'd know within one phone call who it was. That could blow me up or Ava up, and I didn't know if she wanted that. We'd had sex once. The next morning, her life had shattered and well... Why the fuck was I still standing here?

"I gotta go."

"About time you make that decision."

I ignored him, looking for my wallet and keys. We'd just started drinking, so I was still good to drive. "That was...uh—" Where were my keys?

I heard them jangling as Blaise held them up in the air. He dropped his act, getting all serious. "I know who that was. I know what's been happening in her life, and yeah, you dumbfuck, get your ass over there." He tossed them my way and I caught them, but I half-glared at him.

I started for the door.

"Zeke."

I turned back.

He said, a somewhat sad smile on his face, "People care about her."

I reached for the doorknob, and my hand squeezed it tight. "She doesn't think anyone cares about her."

"Then you've got your work cut out for you."

Damn. I loved him for a reason. "Thanks, man." I'd never told him about Ava, but he knew somehow.

He took a long pull from his beer. "Go. No. Wait. Hold up."

"What?" I half-snarled.

He smirked, laughing. "People care about you too, dumbshit."

I snorted. "Love you, man."

"Love you too."

I was out of there after that.

12

AVA

I was in the bath when I heard an abrupt knocking, then shouting, then a crash, then a stampede as someone was running in my apartment. I gasped, starting to jump up just as the footsteps arrived at the bathroom. The door flung open, and Zeke was there, his eyes wild and panicked.

We both stopped in shock, but I remembered I was almost standing up, in my bath, and I was naked. Yes, we'd had sex, but that was in the throes of hotness. Me in the bath, not so much hotness happening here.

I dropped back down, thankful for going crazy with the bubbles, and scowled at him. "What are you doing here? Did you kick in my door?"

"Uh yeah. I owe you a door, but it's okay for now." He was scanning the room, raking a hand through his hair. He didn't answer right away.

"What are you looking for?"

"Booze. I don't know." Not seeing any, his eyes jerked back to me. The wildness had not dissipated. "Are you okay?"

"Yes! I'm in the bathtub." I was seething, embarrassed, and

happy he came over. How messed up was I? "What are you doing here?"

He stepped inside, moving to sit on the closed toilet. He leaned forward, but he wasn't watching me. I could relax a little, moving farther back. He said, "You never text me or call."

I bit down on my bottom lip. Why was my heart skipping a little here? "That's fine. I was..." Terrified. Feeling crazy. "Bored."

His eyes shot to mine and narrowed. "You're lying."

I looked away.

"Look." I could hear him shifting so he could see me more fully. "Blaise is in town. That's the only reason I didn't race over *immediately*, but you sent that one text, and I was already here. If that makes sense?"

It had me feeling a certain way. A good way.

I moved the water around a little. "I didn't mean to interrupt your bromance time with Blaise DeVroe. I know how much you love him."

I risked a look and saw the slight grin on his face. His eyes were firmly trained on where my breasts were located under the water. I sank a little lower, and his gaze jumped back to my face. His grin just widened. "He told me to get my ass over here."

I almost hiccupped. "What?"

"Huh?" His gaze went back to my boobs.

"Zeke!"

"Yeah?" His gaze never moved.

"Your best friend knows about you and me?" And also, what did he know? Thinking on it, what *was* there even *to* know?

"I guess. Screw it." He stood, taking out his phone, his wallet, and his keys. He put them all on the bathroom counter. His shoes and socks were next.

"What are you doing?"

"That's a big tub." His pants came off.

"Zeke!"

His shirt, and whooooooaaaaa... Zeke worked out. Zeke worked out a lot. He was fully muscled, and his stomach was all sorts of hard. I had not fully appreciated his physique during the one time we had sex or the hugs or even the cuddling we did that night. My mouth was salivating because I *was all sorts of* appreciating it now.

He was in the tub in the next second, and I half-shrieked, scooting back as far as I could. It was a big tub, but not that big. Before I could move any more, he reached over, took hold of my waist, and I was lifted in the air, and then he maneuvered us so I was between his legs, my back to his chest, and I could sink down in the water.

Oooooh.

This was... This was amazing, and relaxing, and then his hand began moving over my leg and I was burning up from a whole different reason. "Zeke!"

He chuckled right behind my ear, and even that, with his baritone, sent sensations through me. I didn't know how to handle this, any of this.

"This is way better." He moved again, and I felt him press a kiss to the back of my neck. He began pouring water over me as he kept kissing my neck, his hands beginning to stroke over me at the same time.

If my grandmum were alive and if my mom were still living with me in the house, and this had happened, I would've considered this day heaven. And at the reminders of all the changes in my life, I tensed.

Zeke lifted his head. "What's wrong?"

I sighed, settling back into him. "I wanted you to come over because this is my first night here. I've never not lived with someone—"

His arm muscles bulged, on both arms. He asked, cutting in roughly, "Do you like it?"

"What?"

"Do you like living alone?"

"I haven't experienced it. I can't answer that."

"Move in with me."

"What?!" I jerked forward and twisted so I could see him. As I was learning, Zeke just took care of the problem.

He lifted me up, in all my naked gloriousness, and flipped me around so as I came back down, I was fully straddling him. We both paused at the feeling of him against me, but then I leaned back. "I just moved in here."

He shrugged, his gaze skirting from my mouth to my arm. He began tracing circles on my sides. "You don't like living alone. I didn't know that was the issue." His gaze moved to my eyes. He was somber, almost earnest. "I have that huge house. You could take an entire floor if you want. The basement is renovated to be its own living space. You could have that or the second floor. I don't care. I don't really like living alone either."

I didn't say anything for a moment. "Are you serious?"

He nodded. "I'm always around people, or most of the time. High school, I was always partying. College, I was either at the frat house or I was with Blaise or his brother's group. I bought this house a year ago, and I get it. It sucks living alone. Move in. You can be my roommate."

"You are serious."

A second nod, and his mouth moved into a serious line. "Sex or not, you'd be the perfect roommate. And I mean that. If we're not having sex, that's cool."

"I just moved in. I paid for the first month and I signed a lease."

He leaned back, a cocky smirk appearing. "I know a lawyer. He'll break your lease before he's even had breakfast."

I didn't know who he was talking about, but I was surprised and kinda not at the same time. I let out a short laugh.

"What?"

I shook my head. "You're flashy. I'm not. You live in the fast lane, and me, I'm a tortoise in the slow lane. Sometimes I forget what your life is like when you're with me."

"Ava."

He sounded so serious.

"What?" I asked.

"You're clueless about how many people care about you. I don't know if I should find it adorable or concerning. Or both."

I tensed but shook my head. He was being his crazy self right now.

"How about it?" His hand went to the back of my neck, and as he pulled my head toward his, his hand slid up into my hair. He cupped the back of my head. "Wanna be my roommate?"

My breath caught and held in my chest. That was nuts. Me in Zeke's huge mansion? "You bought that place?"

He nodded, leaning even farther. "Yep. With my own money. No inheritance, nothing from my folks. I think it drove my dad crazy but made him hella proud at the same time. My house is almost as big as theirs."

"What do you do for a job? We've actually never had this conversation."

"I do stocks. I'm a math genius, but no one knows that, and I'm really good at stocks."

I remembered his place.

He was grinning again, eyeing my mouth. "How about it? Roommate?"

I groaned, but I must've made the decision because the resistance was gone.

I'd lived my life a certain way for so long. Living with Zeke, no matter what came, was going to be something so different, I was thinking I was desperate for that change.

"This is insane."

"But?" He looked up, his eyes were dancing. "We can even

give the house a name. Aveke. Ava and Zeke together. How about it?"

"But." Oh God. I *just* moved in. "You have to help me move my stuff."

"I know some people." And as soon as he said those words, his mouth was on mine.

MY EYES OPENED. 3:33 a.m. Zeke had fallen asleep next to me.

I had absolutely no idea what we were doing. I curled up next to Zeke, and he reached for me in his sleep. He tucked me into his side. Sex? Roommates? Were we dating? I hadn't a clue, but I smiled, and my chest felt lighter, and for the first time in a while, I felt the first stirrings of being okay.

I could start to like this a whole lot. I'd worry later if this was either going to shatter me or heal me.

13

AVA

The next morning, he was gone, and I suddenly needed to do something. Anything. I half contemplated running, but I wasn't an exerciser. I was a worker. I worked. That's almost all I did, which was very, very sad now that I was thinking about it.

Getting up, showering, I got ready for the day and headed to the kitchen.

The door was on, and it looked attached, but there was definite damage to it. Zeke had said he'd take care of it, so I wasn't going to stress about it. Yet. Instead, I was going to stress about how he said he wanted me to move in with him.

I couldn't believe he actually meant it. He hadn't. He'd been lying. Just saying things.

God.

Zeke hadn't been lying. He hadn't been saying things. He meant it.

I was going to move in with him.

I was scared if I thought about it, I'd pop like a balloon. A giant Ava-sized balloon. It was starting to rise, looking for the sunshine, smiling, feeling the warmth, and some eight-year-old would come running up and not just to prick the balloon. He'd yank me down, and squeeze, squeeze, squeeeeeze until I popped. Then he'd discard me and run off, laughing because he'd given the world some of his destruction. Joy.

That would happen. I was just waiting for it, but on the bright side, I could enjoy the ride until that happened.

Right?

I wasn't the type to "enjoy the ride." I was the type that if someone was going on a ride, and if their ride went off the rails, I was the bystander that would get hit by the ride. Not them, whoever was in the ride. They'd be fine and dandy. I'd be dead. That was me. That's what would happen. So if it was *my* ride?

I shuddered at the thought of what I couldn't imagine would happen.

That did it. I couldn't move in with him. I'd have to tell him.

He wasn't in the living room or in the kitchen when I left the bedroom, so okay. I checked my phone. No text or message. I looked around. No note left behind.

I brewed coffee. I made toast, ate some fruit, and after that, I waited.

Zeke would come back, maybe expect me to be packing, but I'd tell him then. That I wasn't moving in with him. That it was foolish for me to do that.

I was unpacking the hallway closet when the front door burst open.

"We're here, and tadaa!" Something thumped on the table.

I moved my head, peaking around the pile of blankets. "Zeke?"

"Hey. Yeah. What are you—hold on." He took the pile from me, and glancing around, began to put them on one of the stacks of boxes. As he was doing this, a bunch of guys were filing into my apartment behind him.

One guy walked in, calling out, "Allen—"

Zeke pushed the pile of blankets into the guy's arms. "Here."

"What?" The guy's head popped around them.

"Take those downstairs."

"Zeke—"

But Zeke was already turning and heading my way, some papers in his hands. He held them up for me. "Got you out of your lease."

My lease?

But, I was distracted. Some guys began grabbing boxes and carrying them right back downstairs. One guy stopped and flashed me a smile. "Hey, Ava."

Swear, my knees went weak, but it was Blaise DeVroe. Millions of female knees went weak at just the sight of him. He went into the kitchen, and I heard cupboards being opened.

I was gawking, totally gawking. "What—who are all these people?"

Zeke was giving me a patient but also indulgent smile. "I saw that."

"Saw what?"

"My best friend." He pointed to my stomach. "Did he make your little tummy all fluttery?"

"Oh, my God." I groaned.

He laughed, putting his arm around my shoulders, his side touching right next to my side. "Don't worry. I'm not jealous. I'm very secure in my man-bromances with Blaise and Mason Kade. I'm aware of what a stud my best friend is."

"Shut. Up," came from the kitchen, in a bored deadpan.

Some of the guys who were still carrying what I'd packed snorted, but they never stopped working. A few guys started to grab boxes, ones that I had unpacked the day before and hadn't gotten around to repacking, picked them up, realized nothing was in them, and started packing them.

I was counting twenty guys. At least.

"Look." Zeke nudged me, his head indicating the papers in my hands.

I looked, and then gawked all over again. "What?"

They were my lease papers and I looked at the last one. CANCEL had been stamped over it.

"Told you I could get you out of your lease."

"You called your lawyer friend?"

"No. I didn't need to. Once I looked up who owned this place, it was as good as done."

"Who owns it?"

"My brother-in-law."

Another groan from the kitchen, and a shout, "Nate is *my* brother-in-law, you asswipe." Blaise added a glare as he walked out from the kitchen, out the front door, carrying a box.

Zeke shrugged. "I'm basically adopted into that entire family."

I needed a moment to fully process everything. Guys were walking all around us, and half my stuff was already outside. A couple others began lifting the heavy items as they came in, and they took the kitchen table out. The chairs were next. A whole group began talking about the best way to handle the couch, and I was almost in culture shock. Having help was not in my world. I was so used to doing everything for myself, on my own, for my mom, my grandmother, and now this? With Zeke? I'd barely done a thing, and most of the packing was already done.

Everything I'd unpacked the morning was already in boxes and out of the apartment.

Holy shit. So this *was* happening?

I went to look out the patio door, and saw Zeke's Jeep was being filled up, along with a U-Haul and another truck, that Blaise was shutting its front door. He looked up, saw me, and gave a wave before heading back inside.

"Zeke."

I was remembering back to high school. I'd told Zeke that I had watched him back then, but I was sure he didn't realize how much. Like when I'd waited on him and his friends at Manny's, at the restaurant, the gas station, the pizzeria, all the places. I'd noticed him, and I'd watched. I'd never really been jealous. I didn't like to feel that way, but I had been wistful at times. But Zeke had always scared me. He was big and mean and a fuck boy. Then Blaise had come to town, and Zeke started to change. Blaise brought out another side of Zeke. The changes were little at first, then bigger and bigger until they were past high school, into their college years. And when Zeke would come into Manny's on their holiday breaks, he was almost a different guy. I mean, still Zeke, but...*not* at the same time.

My throat was swelling up because I hadn't fully processed exactly who Zeke was, and him coming into my life. Roommates. Sex. He'd been wonderful after the funeral, before the funeral, and now this? I couldn't comprehend this.

My head was down, folding over. I said again, "Zeke..."

"Hey." Zeke pulled me to the side, then down and into my bedroom. His voice was soft, but his whistle was short and curt to the two guys inside. "Get lost."

They saw me and scrambled.

Zeke shut the door then stood with his back to it. "What's going on?"

I didn't know what to say, how to say it. "This is a lot, and I really appreciate it." My voice was squeaking at the end, and the tears had slipped out. Gah. Tears. I hated them.

"Hey. Hey, hey, hey." He reached for me as he sat on my bed, pulling me into his arms and onto his lap. Reaching up, he brushed some of the tears away before cupping my face in both of his hands. "I'm not sure what this is about, but it's all good. I

sent out a call, and you'll be moved into my place by this afternoon. The lease was no problem. Swear."

"I can't move in with you. This is all, just so—this is all—"

He frowned. "You don't want to move in with me?"

I opened my mouth but froze. Nothing was coming out.

What was I doing? The ride. *Plap*. That'd be me, but he'd
gone and gotten me out of the lease. He had people here. Half
my place was already emptied out. He'd done this. All of this.
And Jarrod. And being there with the move and my grandmum.

I shook my head, whispering, "I don't know what I'm doing
anymore."

"Oh. Ava." He pulled me against him, smoothing a hand
down my back. "You don't have to do anything. Let me handle
it. For real. I got this. I got people for this. I totally got this." His
head inclined. "And for the moving in, we can take it a day at a
time? You'll take the second floor. It's all yours. I already called
to get that cleared away for you. I mean, you're kinda half doing
this for me."

"What?"

His grin was crooked. "I am a very lonely lonely guy."

I started laughing. "You're right. You are."

"I so am. So you moving in is like doing me a favor."

The tightness in my chest began loosening up. Just a bit.
"Well, when you put it like that..." My head was clearing a bit
and I could think more clearly. This was my baggage. Accepting
help. I was starting to get that. I lifted my head until I could
touch my forehead to his. "Thank you. You have no idea how
much this means to me."

His smile turned soft. "Of course. Like I _said, it's no
problem."

For him, it was no problem. He didn't get it, didn't know
how I had grown up, but I didn't want him to get it. That would
bring extra concern for him, worrying about me, and I didn't
want to be anyone's bother. "We're really doing this, huh?"

His hand moved up under my shirt, spreading out over my back. "Fuck yeah, we're doing this. I called all your workplaces and they said you could have tomorrow off too. I was thinking to celebrate, let's do a party tonight?"

"Party?" I stiffened.

He responded right away. "How about a small one? We gotta celebrate you moving in, and my boy is here. He gets like a month off, and with how his family is, I don't know how much time we'll get with him."

But a party? With all his friends?

"What's this about?" He gestured to my face, my frown.

"I don't know who to invite. I don't have a lot of friends."

Zeke started laughing.

"Hey." I scowled at him.

"No. It's—Ava, if only you would realize that you have *a lot* of friends. You don't know they're your friends, but they consider you a friend."

"Oh."

"Leave the party planning to me?"

I nodded. If anything, I could slip away and hide. That was more a me thing to do, but it was his house. Zeke wanted a party. I'd try for him. "That sounds a lot easier."

He started eyeing my shirt, his free hand moving from my leg to pulling it down an inch. "Hmmm. What are your thoughts on quickies?"

My heart sped up. "I've actually never had one."

His eyes lit, and he picked me up. "Never?"

He carried me over, locking the door.

I shook my head. "Nope." I had a feeling that was about to change as he hit the fan. He moved me so I was sitting on top of my desk, and he stepped between my legs. His eyes were all dark, and his mouth lowered to mine.

That was when I also learned that Zeke *really* enjoyed making me scream when I was in a situation where I *couldn't* scream. He was half laughing with his hand covering my mouth as he kept moving inside of me.

I'd say by the end, I was going to enjoy more quickies.

14

ZEKE

It was party time, and the small gathering was...more than small. I stopped counting when it hit in the fifties. Ava looked ready to faint. Which was cute to watch because her eyes had these little crinkle lines around them, and her mouth somewhat turned into fish-lips, which was *fucking* adorable. Her cheeks got a little pink at the top and pale in the middle. And then there was the whole thing where she didn't know what to say or do, and she stood there, like she was frozen in the middle of oncoming traffic.

I could watch her all day long, like right now as she was on the other side of the living room. She got backed into a corner when Blaise's woman and Blaise's brother's woman arrived. They made a beeline for Ava and hadn't left her side.

There was another in that group, but I hadn't seen Blaise's sister show up.

Ava was drinking and kept wetting her lips, which meant she was nervous.

"She's not a big socializer, huh?" Blaise asked, coming behind the bar and leaning against the counter with me. I'd decided to tend bar outside on the patio, with the doors pulled all the way open so the living room and kitchen was free flowing onto the backyard and pool area.

I'd not done much bartending, to be honest. I'd been more fascinated watching Ava. She was like a reality show just for me. I didn't know if that was a good or bad thing, but I also knew a better hunch was not to tell anyone. No one could judge me, and I couldn't stop watching her.

"She thinks she has no friends." We'd gone over this already.

I could feel my bro watch me. I gave him a sideways grin, still not taking my gaze off Ava.

He asked, "And your idea to convince her otherwise was to throw a party?"

"It's a roommate-warming party."

"You stupid."

Now I looked at him, and half-glared, but also half-smirked because that was funny. "You dumb."

"You guys are fucking, right?"

"Tact, buddy. Learn it," I threw back, but I wasn't going to get riled. That was Blaise's specialty. In his heyday, he'd be up and in anyone's face if he felt like it. He was an asshole, but in the best way. I dug it.

"And you're not smart. It's her first night. What are you doing, throwing a party? Ava's always been a loner. This is *not* her scene."

Well.

Shit.

He had a point.

I tore my gaze away and tracked all the people. They were everywhere. I was pretty sure they were in the garage too, which I couldn't blame them. I had some magnificent vehicles, ready for an obsessing audience. Which was why I had them, so people could worship them, because that was the whole point in creating and buying those beautiful pieces of machinery. There was another bar and more games in there as well.

"You think I should invite the Kades? Are they in town?"

Blaise was shaking his head. I could tell from the corner of my eye because I'd gone back to watching Ava. She was so cute.

"Zeke." A guy came up to the counter. "Are you serving drinks?"

I ignored him.

Blaise did too, saying to me, "For your mental health, I'm being a best friend here. Mason Kade does *not* like you."

I just grinned. "I'm wearing him down. We'll be doing holidays with them."

"Allen. Hello." The guy made a motion.

Blaise rolled his eyes. I couldn't see it, but I knew he did as he said, "You might want to start considering something's wrong in your head."

"It's all love, Brother."

"Guys! I want a drink."

We were three feet away from him.

"Maybe we should go over there?"

"To the Kades' house? That would not be a good idea either."

"To Ava." I gave him a look, my eyes flicking upwards. "Who's the Kade-obsessed one *now*?"

The guy said, "You guys are dicks."

Blaise turned on him. "There are like five *fucking* bars in this entire house, his house. Read the silence and go help yourself somewhere *else*."

The guy flicked him off before marching back into the house.

I laughed. "Man, in college, you'd have that guy eating pavement after the first smart comment he made."

Blaise sighed. "You have to be *extremely* professional in my job. That would be unbecoming of me, especially if someone caught it on video. Also, how old are we?"

I snorted. "Never too old for a fun beatdown."

He sighed. "I kinda miss those days. I'm only able to channel that into my playing. The coaches love it."

"And the fans."

"Them too."

We both shared a grin before I went back to my evening's entertainment. Ava. And got a jolt. She was staring at me. I knew I wasn't imagining the fear in her eyes. "I gotta go. My girl's looking ready to panic. Again."

I took my beer, finished it in one gulp, and handed him my empty cup.

Blaise made no move to take it, but I let it go as I started across to her.

Behind me, Blaise cursed then laughed.

15

AVA

I was learning that all those years in high school, there'd been a reason I worked. Other than needing money, and that was because I sucked at socializing. Literally. I'd felt Zeke watching me all night, so that was distraction number one. The other distractions: everything and everyone.

I mean, it was all good things.

I knew this wasn't high school and a "mean girl" wasn't going to come in and make fun of me. That wouldn't happen with Aspen and Bren by my side, who I'd always liked in high school even though I didn't get to know them that well. Well, Aspen. Bren, I knew her a little bit more. Bren was a protector. That's how I thought of her, and when she and Aspen arrived at the party, they'd been trying to be casual, but also mixing in the questions between the normal conversation.

How did this happen?

How was I?

Bren had made a point of being around after my grandmum's funeral. Her sister-in-law owned Manny's so it wasn't a hardship for her to come in there, but I knew she came in a lot more when I was working. She cared. I knew she did. She did the usual, asking how I was, etcetera, but she watched me too. I knew she cared. I knew my bosses cared. What Zeke said, I knew people cared, but I didn't know what was wrong with me. Extreme low self-esteem? Was that it? Or no. It was family stuff. It was because when my dad left, when my mom lost her legs, we were in crisis mode.

Crisis mode. I didn't think I was in it anymore.

Or was I? Did I need to plan accordingly once Zeke got bored with me? Probably, but... I couldn't bring myself to go there. I gave him a look now because he'd not stopped watching me all night, and it was having an effect on me. I was flustered, nervous, awkward, and feeling oddly shy all at the same time. And tongue-tied. Or was that the same thing? Probably the same thing. I'm sure it was.

Bren and Aspen were talking about someone I didn't know when Zeke glided over.

"Ladies." He gave everyone a smooth smile. "You called, my new roommate?"

I frowned. "I did?"

"Your look. It said, 'help me.'" His smile grew. "I'm helping. Whatcha need?" He looked at my drink, and an eyebrow rose. "Another drink maybe?"

"What?" I was mortified, thinking Aspen and Bren would think I needed his help to get away from them. I didn't. I didn't know what I was doing, but his other question threw me, and I looked down. I didn't even know what I was drinking. I hadn't had a sip of it.

"Come on. Let's go." He reached for me, taking the cup first and handing it to Bren.

She gave him a look. "*Excuse* me?"

He only smiled. "You don't have a drink. Take it. You can loosen up a little."

Oh, boy. Bren beat people up for a living. I did not want to mess with her, and when her mouth dropped before she started to get all scarily calm-looking, I darted forward, grabbing Zeke's hand. "Uh. Yeah. Maybe... yeah. Another drink?" I shoved him forward, smiling uneasily over my shoulder at Bren and Aspen behind me. Though, Aspen had her head in her hand and her shoulders were shaking so I didn't think it was as bad of a situation as I thought.

Zeke let me push him a few more feet ahead before he switched places. He began guiding me forward, his arm around me. He bent forward, his mouth teasing my ear. "You've not been around, but you'll find out that I enjoy pissing Monroe off. It's our thing. She'll get all worked up, threaten me, and nothing will happen. Or if something does happen, it's usually between Blaisie and her man."

"You mean Blaise and his brother?"

"Course." He was a little smug as he was maneuvering us past the kitchen, past the other room where a bar was set up, and down the back hall into his primary bedroom.

A couple was kissing on the bed.

Zeke ordered, "Out. Now."

"What?"

The woman scrambled up, hurrying out with the guy moving slower.

Zeke's smile was polite as he said, "Have a nice time, just not in here." The guy threw him a glare, but Zeke dropped the act, letting him see a hardness in him, and the guy hurried out. Zeke glanced my way. "Sorry. I'm all for people enjoying themselves, but one of the rules of partying, you don't take shit when you want shit to happen."

"I know how to handle drunk people."

Zeke was shutting the door, locking it before he looked back, another eyebrow raising up. "I'm sure you do."

"Those people weren't drunk."

"True, but sometimes I like being a dick to people who deserve it. Those two people, they deserved it." He went to a bar that he had in his own room and poured me a drink. "Blaise informed me that maybe I shouldn't have thrown a roommate-warming party on your first night here. Was he right?"

I opened my mouth to tell him no, of course Blaise wasn't right, of course I'd love any party Zeke would throw at his own house, and then realized this was now my home too. Or where I'd be living until something changed, and I relaxed, maybe for the first time since our quickie in my bedroom. I took the glass he handed and went over to his patio door. He had his own sitting area. It was connected to the rest of the backyard, but it was behind a corner. Unless people wandered all the way over to a far corner of the yard, no one would know we were outside.

I opened the door, hearing the sounds of the party already muted from our little area and sat down on one of the lounge chairs. "Is this a party where I need to lock my room?"

Everything I owned was upstairs, still in boxes.

Zeke shook his head. "I went up and locked your door when people started arriving. Most will stick to the basement, main floor, outside, and garage. I've had parties before. Not many venture upstairs, and if they do, usually they see the cameras I have in place."

"You have cameras?"

"Security. I meant to tell you, but we just haven't gotten around to it. It's in the main rooms and hallways. There's none in the bedrooms or bathrooms."

"Good to know."

He was studying me again. Some of the party-Zeke was fading, and I was getting some of my Zeke. He said softly, "I can turn them off when you're here. Turn them on at night or when we're gone, if you want. I'll give you the controls so you can do it yourself, if you want. I don't want you to feel uncomfortable. With the size of the house and because I travel a lot, it seemed smart to have them installed."

That made me feel more comfortable. "You travel a lot?"

He nodded. "At times, or when I want. I can do stocks anywhere."

That was true, and also, a whole new way of living that I wasn't used to. "That's nice."

He frowned a little, and I knew he heard a note in my voice that I wished hadn't slipped out. There was some envy, I couldn't lie about that. Being wealthy had perks. Living was easier, or it seemed that way.

"Wha—" He laughed, a little hitch in there. "I'm sorry. I..." He got all the way serious. "I don't know how to respond to that."

"You don't need to say anything. That's a nice thing you can do, traveling anywhere and whenever you want. But it is a reminder of how different we are. I can't do that. I have to stay where I have a job." I took a sip of my drink, hissing from the vodka's burn.

He nodded, still watching me in his way. "I remember that you were supposed to go to grad school at one point. What happened? Can I ask?"

I needed another drink for that conversation. "Life happened. That's all."

"Ava—"

I looked away, taking a long draw from the drink now. The burn was getting less and less. Thoughts were starting to come in, piling in, but the basic bottom line was: what was I doing? Moving into this giant house? Sleeping with my roommate? He was not in my league. He was so far out of it, skyrocketing out of it, and I knew, even though I'd been fooling myself out in the party, that there would be actual mean girls coming in at some point. Kit. There were others. There had to be. For Zeke to be who Zeke was, of course there'd be bitchy women coming into our lives. My new life? And they'd be there, looking down at me, because who were we all kidding here? I was the help.

I'd be more comfortable being hired to either tend bar at this party or be waitstaff.

A hard laugh rippled up my throat. "What are we doing here?"

"Oh Jesus. Are you serious?" he bit out.

I did a double take, not expecting that from him, and seeing my look, he leaned forward. His own face was hard. "Is this the part of our story where you realize you're poor and I'm not and you decide this is going to go nowhere so you should move right back out?"

His words pierced me, but there was some truth in them. "It would make sense. Yeah..."

He cursed. "Fucking please." He stood up, going back into the room and added to his drink.

"You're mad? At me?"

He didn't answer, but his eyes were trained right on me as he came back outside, sitting down in the chair beside me.

I asked, "Is this our first fight?" I was in the twilight zone. We'd only fucked twi—more than twice, more than three, four actually, but this was happening too fast. Way too fast. I should've known. I began to stand up.

"Where are you going?"

"Leaving. You're right. I shouldn't be here."

His eyes were angry, blazing. "I didn't say that. I said that's what *you* were going to say."

I couldn't deny that. "It's true. I mean, what is this? What are we doing? I didn't even ask about rent. I have no idea if I can pay for it."

"You really think I'd make you pay me rent?"

I flushed. "You better! I'm not a freeloader. I have *never* been one."

"Maybe that's part of the problem."

I fell silent. My whole insides were twisted up. "What does that mean?"

He half-glared at me, taking a pull from his drink.

"Zeke. What does that mean?"

He still didn't answer, taking another draw from his drink. Still glowering too.

"Zeke Allen, answer me right now." I would've folded my arms over my chest if I didn't have a drink, so I folded one arm across my chest and tried to look intimidating.

"I want you with me, and I'll keep saying it as many times as you need me to hear it." He sighed. "You look at me like that, and all I'm thinking is how I want to throw you on the bed, peel off your pants, and sink so far inside of you that you forget everything we were just talking about."

My body got insta-hot. Like, heated to boiling hot.

And, well, damn.

"What?" I could only mutter, feeling the throb burst deep inside for him.

He saw it. He did. He knew the effect he had on me, and just like that, the whole feel of the conversation turned. It took a one-eighty, and he was giving me a wolfish look, one that had my toes curling, and I could only let out a shaky sigh because I knew he was two seconds away from doing just what he said he wanted to do.

I was going to let him, because as he finished his drink, set the glass aside, and started for me, I knew without a doubt that Zeke Allen had buried himself deep inside of me and I had no idea what to do about it. He stepped to me, his hand moving around my neck, cradling the back of my head, he must've hit a button because privacy slides were rolling down over his windows, and I groaned right before his mouth fell on mine.

After that, he did exactly what he promised.

I loved every second of it.

16

AVA

I t'd been a month, and well, I knew two things. One, I wasn't paying rent. Every time I asked, Zeke tried to have sex with me. He mostly won those conversations. And two, I had never understood the sex-obsessed people. The girls who gushed about it in Manny's at night. The books. The movies. Society.

I did now. Oh, boy, did I understand now.

The other thing I didn't know, was how my bed felt because I hadn't slept in it. Every night, we were in Zeke's. If I informed him I was going to my room, to my bed, somehow I'd still end up in his. He was damned good at it too.

I was just coming from the back section at Manny's when I heard Zeke's voice from the bar area. Since I moved in, he'd come in a few times, but not as much as before. Though he and I were... well, he and I. I'd missed seeing him at Manny's. There was comfort in familiarity, and Brandon clocked me coming from the back. He pulled his hand back, and I rounded the bar, pouring Zeke's beer myself. I flashed Brandon a grin. "We're not that busy. You can take off if you want?"

He glanced around. I wasn't lying. We weren't busy, but I

still had six hours before closing, and there wasn't another bartender on staff. "I'll stay till ten, how about?"

"Okay." I slid Zeke's beer across the bar to him. "Hey."

His hand closed over it, over mine before I pulled back. "Hey."

Brandon was watching us, and chuckled. "Look at you two."

Zeke shot him a look, tipping his head back.

Oh, no. I recognized that look. It was the one where he wasn't sure if Brandon was being nice or not, and he was going to bait him to see what reaction he got. Yeah. That was another thing I knew about Zeke.

He wasn't the simple guy most considered him as. He was layered, and he kept most under the surface, packed under the smiling and charming jackass he could be at times. Case in point as I was bracing myself for what he was going to say to Brandon.

He delivered, "Look at us...what? You got something to say to back that up or just that, 'look at them' and see how the room is going to react?"

There was some bite to his voice.

Brandon stopped drying a glass, lowering the towel. "You kidding? What's that about?"

Zeke leaned forward. "I think that's the point *I'm* making. What's your comment about? You and me, we're friendly from a distance. We aren't buds where I can shrug off some needling. The question I have for you is what are *your* intentions? Friendly or public mockery?"

There was a lot more bite to that comment.

Brandon stood back, his whole face in shock, and I understood. He knew this side of Zeke existed. I knew too, but he hadn't seen it in a while except when a female got too persistent and wasn't taking a hint.

Brandon shook his head, slowly, flicking his gaze my way before snorting. "Nice to see you haven't changed, Allen." He motioned to me. "I'm taking five." He gave Zeke a tight look passing by me and heading down the back hallway.

I moved in, frowning. "Did you have to go that hard?"

Zeke leaned back, the tension gone and picked up his beer. "He was walking the line between being kind or making us a joke. Now, he won't make us a joke."

Well, there was that. "You don't know he would've done that."

"Yes," Zeke said it tightly. "He would've because he doesn't like me. He doesn't like me for you. And he doesn't have the place to step forward and warn me off. That was his way of broaching that gray area, but I gave him something to actually bitch about. Except now, he'll be more careful about choosing his words and what message he's going to deliver."

Some customers came in, so I moved to handle their drinks. When I got back to Zeke, he was watching Javalina again. I frowned. "I didn't know they were playing again. I thought they were off-season now?"

"It's a rerun."

"Oh, gotcha." Still. "Who do you know on their team?" I'd always wondered because he tended to know quite a few professional athletes.

He frowned back at me.

I grinned. "What? You rotate between Blaise's team, Mason Kade's team, the Kansas City Mustangs hockey team, and the Javalina hockey team. You watch the Javalina more than the Mustangs, so I can't quite figure out if you know someone on the Mustangs' team or just like them, but I know you know someone on the Javalina because you watch them almost as much as Mason Kade's team. So." I propped my hip against the counter. "Who is it?" I thought about it. "Please tell me it's not someone who is currently screwing someone you used to screw?"

He cracked a grin. "I don't know anyone who plays for the Mustangs, but I like Cutler Ryder."

One of my guesses was answered. "And the Javalina?"

"I know one of the guys. He's in a relationship with a friend of mine."

I raised an eyebrow. "Did you screw this friend?"

"No." His lips twitched again. "She and I were not like that."

She. I knew it'd been a she. "Are you going to tell me her name?"

He was full on grinning at me now. "I'm kinda liking you not knowing. You're getting heated. I like this reaction. Are you jealous?"

I growled, but more customers came in, and I went to help them out.

After that, we got swamped. Four baseball teams decided Manny's was their new hangout after their games, and I was thankful Brandon had decided to stick around. I also forgot all about the Javalina and Zeke's friend too, that was, until around midnight when I looked over and saw a different friend standing next to him. Standing real close to him.

Penny Lancaster. I didn't know if she was married, or if she was, what her married name was, but my stomach shrank because I remembered how he and Penny were on-and-off again in high school. She'd been more than a one-night thing, and dammit, but I knew this. I so knew this. This was not a secret. He had a past, a big past, and who was I to even get worked up about it? We were sleeping together and room-mates, but beyond that, I hadn't a clue. We'd not had "the talk," hashing out if we were exclusive or not, but then again; when would that have come into play? I was the one who left for work, but when I wasn't, Zeke was around. All the time. In the house, or in another room, or at Manny's.

And now with Penny.

My head was spinning, and this wasn't good.

I shouldn't be reacting this way, but I couldn't stop or ignore the burn that was going down my chest.

I went over to them, and wished that she had aged bad, but she hadn't. She still looked as beautiful as I remembered from back then, one of the popular girls from their rich private school.

He lifted his head up as I neared them. "Hey."

Penny had started to speak, seeing me, but hearing his tone, how he greeted me, she gave me a whole different look. Her eyes got sharper. Her mouth closed a little before she had a fake smile on her face and raised her chin up a little. A Lana Marks Cleopatra Clutch in her hand. "Hi..." She cocked her head to the side. "You're Ava, right? From Roussou?"

I flashed her a thin smile. "I am. What would you like to drink?"

I felt Zeke watching me and ignored him.

Her eyes narrowed before another smile smoothed out over her face, and she pulled out the chair beside Zeke. "How about your most expensive wine?" She slipped onto the seat, and her smile got brighter. Her eyes slid toward Zeke. "On this guy?" She playfully elbowed him.

That burn started digging right down and deep into me, going faster. "Sure." I didn't wait for Zeke to approve, and turned, reaching for the good stuff. The most expensive stuff because that's who she was. She was worth the pricey stuff. Not me. I was worth the cheap stuff. The beer on tap. Jell-O shots. That was me. And this chick, Penny Fucking Lancaster, the ex or the one who could've been considered the ex of Zeke's if he ever had a steady girlfriend because she was it. The one who was mostly on-and-off with him, and that said a lot about her, about what she meant to him.

And I was totally and irrationally jealous, and I hated this feeling. The burn was hurting, slicing into me.

I poured the wine and slid the glass over to her. "Raise a

hand when you need a refill." Still ignoring Zeke, I walked right past Brandon and said under my breath, "I'm taking five."

I felt Zeke's eyes on my back as I kept going, right out the side door.

If I smoked, I would've been smoking. I didn't, so instead, I was perched on a picnic table in the back and bent over, looking at my phone. It buzzed, but I ignored Zeke's text.

And his next two until I put my phone away because he was now calling me.

A second later, he stepped outside, his phone to his ear, and seeing me, he put it away. "What is going on with you?"

I glared at him. "If you were to guess?"

His eyebrows bunched together. The sides of his mouth turned down. "I'm actually lost here." He stepped down the stairs but put his hands in his front pockets. He stopped right in front of me, his head lowered, his eyes trained on me. "Connect the dots, please. I don't like feeling lost when it comes to you."

"Are you serious? I know who that is."

"Penny?" His confusion seemed to double.

"I know she was your fuck buddy back in school."

Understanding dawned, but then his face went blank, really fast. I didn't like the "really fast" part because he was hiding it now, from me. "That was a long time ago. You want me to be an ass when your ex shows up?"

I gave him a look. "You would, and we both know it. You already were with Jarrod."

His shoulders relaxed a little. "Yeah. You're right. I was a dick to Brandon and he just said, 'you two.'"

I almost grinned at that, or I would've, if I wasn't still mad at him. Mad because he had an ex who was inside, who I had to give "the really expensive stuff" to. I had to say it. "She is not worth that wine, just saying."

A gentle grin came over him, and he took a step closer, his head lowering even more. "You're right. She's not."

I waited for the line, waited for him to say that instead, I was worth it. But he didn't, and I glanced up.

He'd been waiting, the side of his mouth curved up. "I know what you're thinking."

I laughed, reaching out to shove him back, not thinking about it. He caught my hand instead, and he used it to haul me up as he surged forward. We were hugging, and I didn't push him away. My hand curled in on his shirt, holding him in place. He tipped his head back, still smiling at me, as his hands wrapped around me and slid down, moving up under my shirt. "You like me. Like, *like*-like me."

I looked away. "Shut up."

"You do. You totally do." He began to rock us back and forth, his hands sliding up against my back.

A tingle raced up my spine from his touch, but I half scowled at him. "We're sleeping together. Of course, I like you, you idiot."

He stopped rocking us and his forehead moved down, resting on mine. I could feel him getting serious and held my breath. He said, almost quietly, "I like-like you too. Like, like like like like you."

A slight laugh escaped me. "You are not funny. That's not something to laugh at."

"You're the one who just laughed."

"Because you said you 'like like like' me."

"No." He was still serious. Almost solemn. "I said that I 'like like like like' you."

"Such a difference."

"It is. There's a lot of difference between like like like and like like like liking someone. I like like like like you and I might even go so far to say that I like like like like *like* you, a lot."

"You can be kinda..." I was going to say stupid, but he wasn't. He was being sweet and funny, and he was making me smile. And he didn't care that I'd been irrationally jealous seconds ago.

"What? I can be what?" His hand was moving over my back, sensually.

I was really starting to like like like like *like* how he was touching me.

I shook my head. "Intense sometimes, and sweet at other times."

His head lifted, but he kept studying me. "Is that an okay thing?"

I nodded. "That's an okay thing." My break was almost done. "I need to go back in. Can you do me a favor?"

"Anything."

I gave him a look.

He just grinned back at me.

"Can you put an entire seat between you and your ex?"

He laughed but nodded. "I can do you better. How about I put an entire building between myself and her?"

I stilled. "What?"

"She took off."

"What?"

"As soon as you left, I took the wine and told her there's no fucking way I was spending that much money on her ass."

A surprised laugh caught in my chest.

He smirked. "You are just not getting it."

"Getting what?"

His eyes flashed, fierce, for a second. "That there is no one in my past you need to worry about. No one. Literally. The only one I've come to care about..." His hand reached up and touched a strand of my hair, tucking it behind my ear. "...is you."

Warmth burst inside of me, and oh boy. I recognized that feeling. It was way beyond all the likes put together.

17

ZEKE

A month later

I liked baseball. I played at Cain University for my last two
years. It was nothing serious, more something for me to do
and another reason for the fraternity to celebrate something,
but I liked it. It was my thing, kinda. Not counting the guys in
the frat, all of my friends had their own things. Blaise had
soccer. Well, all of Blaise's family and their significant others
had their own groups.

I liked sex. Being a social butterfly. I was the glue that
connected people, brought people together. Sometimes I got
sticky and was walked on, and I knew that part. I was okay with
that. No one thought of me as that, but I knew it. Like I was the
sidechick for my buds. I said the funny thing, or the mean
thing, and people either laughed at me or they got mad at me,
but they didn't understand that I was the spark.

I made things happen. Someone needed a push? I did it.
Someone needed to be checked up on? I did it. The only real

time I got nervous was when Blaise wanted to do something to one of my frat bros, and I was like, "Uh, I don't know, bro." And he was like, "We're doing it." And then I was like, "Okay." And I did it because that's what I did.

I was the support. That was my role. Supporting my friends to shine and do their thing. Though, I'll admit that I didn't accept that role until Blaise came back to Fallen Crest. But I needed it. I was lost and wandering, and I wasn't going to turn into a good guy. I knew that much. I was the dude that did better with structure. Blaise came in, and he became a part of my structure, and it was up to me to give myself the other part of my structure. Later, my dad *really* gave me structure, and that changed my outlook on everything.

I'd always be grateful, but still, through college, I was the support for everyone. They just didn't know it. Then we graduated and everyone went on to their lives. Their careers. I figured out my way, though it was hard at times. I felt that old lost feeling again, and it really sucked for a bit. That's when I started playing baseball at Cain, and that helped again.

So that's what I did again, except I was playing softball for the Kade Enterprises Team. Not baseball. It was made up of a bunch of their employees, and a couple of the board members. My dad had been on it first until he got hurt and asked me to take his place.

Doing stocks was well and good, but I didn't have a lot of people in the area. Or like family people. I had a lot of people who knew me, who I knew, who thought we were friends, and we were, but... not the kind that I considered family. The kind that really knew me. Blaise was in Europe. Mara was in another state. My dad retired and he and my mom now traveled in an RV. My mom loved it because she could drink and sleep in the back, and my dad loved it because he could act like he's poor. Legit. He took a picture of a bunch of ramen that they were eating for the week. In all honesty, I thought it was making my dad happy again, and he told me that my mom wasn't drinking as much. But they were gone, and in Alaska. They had a whole pitstop in Canada. I had no clue why, but the pictures looked very marijuana happy so good for them.

But... the last couple years, I'd been in one of those 'lost' phases again.

The softball playing helped, but it was just a night every third Thursday of the month. We weren't a team that played weekly or biweekly. But I was at our game tonight.

Ava was working at Manny's, and I had plans to head there after the game.

We were playing against the Fallen Crest Bankers Association team, who was like us. They only played once every third Thursday, and so far, it wasn't much of a game. They had a couple young players who knew what they were doing. I was guessing they were roped in, new tellers or something, but the older players—I was fairly certain they were playing with their kids' gloves, if that's an indication what kind of team they were.

We were nearing the ninth inning, and I was surprised it hadn't been called. We were twelve to one, and the one was walked. I was on deck, so I had my bat, but I didn't need to warm up.

"Hey, Zeke." The first baseman's ref came over. I had to think, placing him, and grunted hello when I did. He was on the board at Fallen Crest Financial City, had a boy in high school, a girl in college. His wife used to hit on me every Tuesday night at Manny's.

"Roger."

His eyes lit up. He liked that I knew his name.

"Heard you got a lady. Is that true?"

A lady? I grinned at the terminology but nodded. "Yep. I do."

"That Ava girl, right?"

I frowned, just a little. In general, dudes didn't bring up

another dude's woman unless there was a reason. And if that happened, usually the reason wasn't a good one, or it was going to go in a not-good place. I was waiting for Roger to tell me which way this conversation was going to go.

"Uh huh."

He nodded, a little bit too eager for my liking. "She's a pretty one. Her mother is staying at a facility where my girl volunteers. Says Ava comes in and sees her mom every other day. Does lunch with her before she goes off to her job at Manny's. I always thought it was a shame that she'd not gotten scooped up by someone. Girl like that. Pretty. Quiet. Real pretty. Hard worker too."

I was starting to see where this conversation was going to go. The more he talked, the more eager I was getting for that end result. "Really."

"Oh, yeah." There it was, a nice dirty gleam in his gaze. He licked his lips and hitched up his pants. Bending over, peering at home plate, he shook his head. "I gotta ask—"

I grunted, "No, you don't."

"—what's she like in bed, man—"

He didn't heed my warning.

He kept on, but I stopped listening because I'd heard enough to hear him talk about shit he shouldn't be talking about. Bed. Positions. Energy. How her legs felt wrapped around me.

All calm-like, as the batter struck out and I was up, I tossed my bat in the air.

Roger was still talking.

I had a fleeting thought that it would've been nice if Blaise was here for back-up, and I caught the end of my bat and swung, just like I was going to hit a grounder. A nicely aimed grounder where I still had follow-through, but the ball was directed to hit immediately down but with a bounce. Not where I took the bat and bunted. Not that kind, because that wouldn't have been satisfactory, but this guy, this Roger, he should've heeded my warning.

My woman. She didn't deserve to be talked about like that, and as I swung, as I clipped him clear across in the face, I heard yells in the distance. There was a whistle sound. People were shouting. Then running. Roger was on the ground. I got him clean, not in the front, to the side. I'd aimed it just right, but he was bleeding and he was unconscious, and my teammates were shoving me backwards.

His team members were up in arms, yelling.

Someone was threatening me. More than one, actually.

I didn't care. I walked backwards, letting my teammates push me back, but I kept watching Roger. If he woke, I wanted to see him. I wanted his eyes on me.

"What the fuck, Allen?! Why'd you clock him?"

"He was disrespecting Ava." Seemed simple to me.

My teammate swore. "Cops are coming. That's Roger Mitchell. He could sue you."

I dug into my wallet, and pulled out a card, handing it up. "Call my lawyer."

He cursed again, but took it, and swore a third time. "Logan Kade?"

I grinned. "Something tells me he'll be happy to represent me. Make sure to tell him the reason."

He shook his head but took the card. He was pulling his phone out as a squad car was turning into the softball fields. I knew the officers who were getting out of the car, and as one headed my way, the other one cut across to check on Mitchell.

"What the fuck, Zeke?"

I grinned. "Still think it's funny you decided to go law enforcement after college, Ryerson."

Race Ryerson shook his head at me, his mouth all tight-lipped as he liked to get when he was worked up. I knew him

from when we were in high school, but the better connection
was because he'd married Blaise's sister.

He sighed. "It was this or doing custom race cars."

"No. I think it's funny considering your family lineage."

His partner was coming over, shaking his head. I also
knew him from high school. Branston Strandling. Before
Blaise, he and his brother were considered my closest friends.
He cursed at me. "Why'd the fuck you do that? They're saying
you just all-out swung on him? He wasn't even looking at
you."

"He was being disrespectful toward Ava." I gave him a
warning look because his brother had been close to doing the
same not that long ago as well.

He stilled but swore under his breath. He got the look. "Brian's an asshole."

"You're considered an asshole as well."

Race cursed. "Zeke. My God."

Branston shot back. "Fuck you, Zeke. You were the king of
assholes back then."

"Hence, why I swung. I'm also loyal and in love with Ava—"
I stopped because holy fuck. I blinked a few times, letting the
surprise filter through me. I was in love with Ava. I—I'd never
loved a chick before.

Both guys had quieted, watching me.

Race asked, quietly, "First time realizing?"

"Yeah." I blinked some more and held out a hand. "Holy
fuck. I think I have to sit down."

Branston snorted, but the ambulance was turned in, lights
all flashing. We watched as the paramedics rolled up, went over
and checked on Mitchell, and it wasn't long before he was put
on their stretcher and they loaded him up into the wagon. One
of the paramedics came over, grimacing. "He's going to have a
concussion. You got his teeth, so there'll be dental work." He
gave me a pitying look. "He's talking lawyers already. Sorry,

man." He gave a small wave to us. Race lifted his chin in a salute, but Branston was looking my way.

"We'll need to arrest you."

I gave him a look, still dazed from my realization. "The world is brighter. Is that normal? Maybe I'm in shock too."

Race wheezed out a laugh before coughing, covering it up. A couple of Mitchell's teammates came over. One was scowling. "That was a very stupid—"

I growled. "Get lost, Ditterson. He was talking dirty about my woman. And if you think I'm not going to fight him because of that, you're a moron."

He stopped talking. The guy next to him drew up as tall as he could. He tugged at his shirt. "What—uh—what do you mean by that?"

I wasn't caring that I was in the presence of two cops as I swung my gaze now his way. I fixed both with looks of frustration. "If you think I grew up in Fallen Crest, in the belly of the white-collar crime part of it, that I didn't take note of every dirty thing you all have done over the years? And that I didn't keep it put away in a nice folder somewhere, then you deserve what I'm going to let loose on Mitchell. My father was on the board of Kade Enterprises. He used to golf with you dirtbags. He ain't stupid. Neither am I."

"How would you know—" He shut up, remembering who else was standing beside me, wearing badges.

"Because I'm good with numbers, stocks, and computers. And no one knows that about me, except Blaise."

Race looked my way.

Branston pulled out his cuffs and held them up in the air. "Do us a favor and walk away?"

They snapped their attention to him. One snipped, "You just remember to do your job. You work for us, you know."

Branston's tone was tight. "We'll do our jobs." They walked off, and he swung to stand in front of me, blocking their view.

"You're going to put cuffs on me?"

His eyes were flat. "Fuck no, but those pieces of shits have to think I am."

"Hey." My teammate hurried over, holding out the card that I gave him. "I got a hold of your lawyer."

"Yeah?"

"I told him what you said, and he said it's no problem. Anything for Ava or Nate's adopted son."

I laughed.

My teammate frowned, confused.

"Is he flying in?"

"He's in the area. He can meet you at the station." He scanned Race and Branston. "I'm assuming that's where you're going, right?"

Branston sighed. "Yes. We're here to do our jobs. An assault happened, so we'll be taking him in."

My teammate gave a nod before joining the rest of the team.

Race asked, "What about your car?"

I shrugged. "I can get it later." But I was seeing how he was studying it and remembered his other vocation he'd considered once upon a time. "You mentioned custom race cars?"

"My dad had a shop, worked on bikes, but I don't know. I always liked the car part of it."

"If you ever think of doing that, I'll invest."

His attention jerked back to me. "Yeah?"

I nodded, knowing what my gut was telling me. "Yeah."

"Thanks, Zeke. I might take you up on that offer."

"Okay, *chicas*, not to break up your future business deal, but we need to go." Branston held his hand out to me. "Give me your keys. I'll drive it to the station for you."

I handed them over. "Thanks, man."

Branston jerked his head toward their squad car. "Pretend you're handcuffed and get inside."

I opened my mouth.

He shook his head. "And don't be a smartass. We both know it's not the first time you've been in the back of a cop car."

I couldn't help myself. "First time where you're supposed to be in the driver's seat."

He snorted, before shaking his head and heading off to my vehicle.

Race drove instead, and once we were on the way, he glanced back in the rearview mirror. "You're really in love, Zeke?"

I could let myself think about it, about what I did, what I had no problem doing, and what I'd do again, all because he was talking dirty about my woman. It wasn't my first time in a fight. Hell. Blaise used to start fights all the time and I'd wade in, but how it happened, how I just swung without batting an eye, that was out of the ordinary for me. Or it was now.

"Yeah, man." Ava. Just the thought of her was making me smile. "I'm in love."

I grunted, letting my head fall back against the headrest. "Fuck."

18

AVA

*Z*eke never showed. Some of his teammates came into Manny's, gave me looks, but remained on the restaurant side of the place. I frowned but kept working, though I checked my phone. Zeke had said he was going to come over after their game. There were no calls, no texts.

It was a little after ten when the side door opened, and in came Heather Jax, or Monroe since she'd taken her husband's last name. She wasn't alone. Her alone wouldn't have sent alarms going through me since she was my boss, had been in some varying way since I was a teenager. She owned Manny's along with her brother, but she came in, saw me, and headed right for me. Behind her was her sister-in-law, Bren Monroe.

Bren was also one of the most beautiful women I'd known growing up, with dark hair, large doe-like eyes. I knew she had a reputation of being fierce and primal, like a wolf, which had been what her crew was once called. The Wolf Crew. I went to school in Roussou, but I'd not been a part of the crew system.

She and Heather together made sense. They were family. Heather owned the place. No reason for alarm...but they weren't alone. Tasmin Ryerson was also with them. Blaise's sister. She was the other brother's twin, but all three of them shared the same good looks. Tawny hazel eyes. Naturally tan. Beautiful golden blonde hair.

All three together, all three looking my way, and my heart sank a little.

Zeke and I were together. There'd been no official conversation, but I knew we were. I'd accepted it. There'd been no need for me to worry about exclusivity. Zeke had made it clear he only wanted me, but besides knowing Bren, Tasmin, and Heather in different ways, I wasn't really 'in' their group.

My core had been my ex, my mom, and my grandmother. There'd been one other girl that I sometimes went to a movie with, but she moved away a long time ago. I was digressing. I was trying to say that I wasn't a casual friend type of person. It was fine. It was how I was, and I fully knew that Zeke was more in this group than I was. They all liked him, put up with him at times, but since high school, they had adopted him. Or he made them adopt him, which was probably more the way of it and now I was with Zeke, so I'd been wary about telling any of them.

It just felt weird. I didn't know my place anymore. Bren, that was easier because she wasn't around that much anymore, but Heather was. Brandon wasn't a fan of Zeke and since he was Heather's brother, and I knew they were tight, I'd been well, I'd been quiet about my relationship. Though, I adored Heather. *Adored* her. I'd do almost anything for her. She'd given me so much over the years. I'd never be able to repay her kindness. And knowing all of that, knowing Zeke and I had been together for a while, and seeing her giving me a look, my stomach was doing a tango.

I was thinking 'the talk' was about to happen.

"Ladies." I was the only one manning the bar tonight. Derek had left twenty minutes ago. "What would you like to drink?"

"We're not here to drink."

Bren was the one who spoke, but Taz raised her hand. "I am. I'm here to drink. Can I get a vodka spritzer, please? Thank you."

Heather was looking around. "We're busy. You're alone tonight?"

I was reaching for the vodka and the cranberry juice as I nodded. "I'm okay. I can handle the bar."

"Derek left?"

I nodded as I made up the drink, glad I'd already cut new mint leaves ten minutes ago. I was swirling everything together, a couple strawberries thrown in as I asked Heather, "Sure you don't want anything?"

"Uh." She was eyeing the glass as I handed it over to Taz, whose eyes were lit up. "Actually, that looks good."

I gave a nod, reaching to do another and glanced at Bren. "You sure?"

She gave a nod. "Just give me a water."

"Water coming up."

As I finished Heather's drink and poured Bren her water, I kept watching them. They weren't talking, but all three were on their phones. That's when I felt my own phone buzz in my pocket. *Finally.* It was Zeke. He was going to tell me he'd stayed late to chat with someone and was heading over now. He'd apologize for not texting sooner.

That's what I was expecting as I slid both drinks over the counter to them and began to reach for my phone.

Bren said, curtly, "Don't do that."

I paused, my eyebrow going up. She had a very serious look on her face. Taz was watching her, watching me, but closed her mouth over her metal straw and took a sip. A long sip. Heather was frowning at her own phone. "What the hell?"

And that was my question too, because this couldn't be good. None of it.

My whole stomach just shrank in size. I braced myself.

"Was he in an accident?" The elephant in the room had been acknowledged.

Taz started coughing, spitting out her drink.

Bren's eyes got big. "No. Oh, no. Nothing like that."

Heather was giving me a grim face.

I kept cutting to her. "What? Just tell me. What is it? What happened?"

She hesitated, and this was Heather Jax. She never hesitated. Ever. She was the queen of kicking ass, I mean, after Bren. They were both up there, taking no bullshit. Bren was in an actual fisticuffs way, but you still didn't mess with Heather Jax. She'd cut your balls off.

But the hesitation did me in, and I whipped out my phone.

"Ava—" Bren started to stand up from her stool.

I turned my back and read the text that was just sent through.

Unknown number: This is Zeke. I got arrested. I'm fine. Lawyer Kade should get me out soon. Don't worry about me. I swung on someone, but there was reason. Don't let anyone twist it, please. Let me tell you what happened first.

I texted back:

Me: Whose phone is this?

Unknown Number: This is his lawyer. Working on bail.

My God. Bail.

He swung on someone? What did that mean?

Unknown Number: Don't talk to anyone. That's imperative.

I frowned. Talk to no one?

"What did that just say?" Bren had come around to my side of the bar, and she was looking at my phone.

I put it away, even warier because I liked Bren. Like I said, she'd been a sort of protector of mine, but I backed away. "I—it was his lawyer. I'm not supposed to talk to anyone."

"Who's his lawyer?"

I glanced at Heather, who was finishing her drink. She looked concerned, but also not that concerned because she was looking at her drink like she'd just discovered chocolate for the first time.

"It said Lawyer Kade. I—I'm not sure who that is."

Heather's head jerked up. "Logan?"

"Wait." Tasmin shot a hand up, her drink done and pushed over for a second. "Logan Kade is in town?"

She and Bren looked in Heather's direction, which made sense since Heather was friends with the Kades. Her husband was also really good friends with Mason Kade, Logan's brother. Both were well-known in the area, considered legendary by some. Lord knew, I was aware how much Zeke was fan-obsessed with Mason Kade. He told me one night that he kept a picture of him in his locker in high school.

I laughed so hard that I had to run to the bathroom.

Heather looked startled. "I—uh—" She laughed, a sheepish grin showing. "I'm sorry, but I'm so distracted." She picked up the glass. "This is the best drink ever, and I know the recipe, but you added something extra to it. What did you add?"

Some of my tension eased a little. "I'm not telling my secret."

She shook her head, a slight laugh coming from her. "I could drink seven of these in thirty minutes. This is *that* good. Ava, you're like magic. Pure liquor magic."

More of my tension eased again. "Thanks, Heather. Means a lot coming from you."

"Can we keep to the issue at hand. Zeke's in jail, and we were sent to help you."

"Help me?" That ball just wound back up again. "What do you mean?"

"The fight was over you."

"Bren!" Taz said.

"Over me? *What?* What do you mean?"

"It's all fine." Heather finished her drink and pushed it over to me. "Give me a refill, please."

"Me too!" Taz grinned, holding her glass up.

"Guys."

"It's fine, Bren." Heather shook her head. "Logan's here. Logan's on the case. Logan will get him out."

Bren snorted. "You might think Logan Kade is a god, but I don't. With what Race said, the case is clear cut. Open and shut. Zeke full out just took a bat to the guy."

"What?" I almost shrieked now. Because, what the hell? "What happened?"

Bren gave me another grave look. "That's the other reason we're here. You and Zeke. Your relationship."

Taz held a hand up. "Um, I like their relationship. Zeke is different with Ava."

Bren looked her way. "Zeke's slept with almost all of my friends, excluding you. And he would've slept with you if you hadn't already been dating Race."

"Those were Aspen's friends from college, but yes. I see your point. You made other female friends later, and he did sleep with them."

My stomach was now like a rock.

Taz kept talking. "But he loves her. He said it tonight."

I'd been holding a glass, prepared to dip it in for some ice, but those words—I dropped it.

Heather gasped, lurching upright.

Bren frowned.

Taz's eyes got wide, and she stopped talking. "Oh—oh no. I just let it slip."

Zeke...

I reached out, grabbing the counter.

Zeke loved me?

I whispered, "What did you say?"

Heather held her hand out. "Guys, it's fine. It's all fine. Zeke, that's for him to say." She focused on me. "We don't know what triggered Zeke, but the guy has turned his life around. He's a good guy. I can't believe I'm saying that, but he is. If Logan is his lawyer, one, that's shocking enough since he lives on the east coast, but I know Logan. If he's here and he's handling Zeke's case, there's a reason. Zeke will be fine." She swung around, giving Bren a meaningful look. "They'll take care of it."

Bren narrowed her eyes. "They'll make it go away?"

"Probably, but Zeke will be fine."

I had to take a step back, still dazed.

Bren bent down and scooped up the glass. It hadn't shattered since it was made up from some special kind of material. It only bounced on the rubber floor we had under the bar, put in place for this very reason. As she put it in the sink to get rewashed, Heather let out a breath of relief. "Oh, good. In her state, I was worried she'd cut her hand or foot or something."

"Huh?"

Zeke was in love with me...

Bren noted my state and grunted. "She's in shock. Who am I kidding? I'm in shock too. Zeke Allen? In love? He's been a pain in my ass—"

"Don't."

She quieted, going still at my command.

I blinked, feeling a weird sensation coming over me, like new skin. But I had to back it up even against Bren Monroe. "Don't talk about him that way." I took a step back, just in case, but my whole body was shaky. "He's—he's not that guy anymore."

Taz added, quietly, "He hasn't been for a long time."

"I know, but he still needles me."

"That's you. Zeke's been different for a long time, since high school."

"I know that too."

Zeke was in love with me.

The information just kept swimming in my head.

I couldn't believe it.

But he'd stood up for me how many times?

He came to my place, worried.

He broke into my place.

He got into the tub with me.

He moved me into his place.

He told his ex to stuff it.

He—I loved him too.

I loved Zeke Allen,

But, God.

I think I fell in love with him a while ago.

"I love him," I said it quietly, to myself, but I lifted my head up.

Heather, Bren, and Tasmin were all focused on me. A gun could've gone off, and I didn't think they would've looked away.

I swallowed over that lump, making it go away. "I don't care what he did. I'm sure he had reason. I love him." I turned to Bren. "Oh, my God. Is this bad? This is bad, right? I shouldn't be in love with him, but wait." I remembered what Taz said.

He said he loved me, and Zeke didn't lie.

He didn't lie.

Bren moved in closer, her hand coming to my shoulder. "Should you, maybe, uh... Heather?"

"What's up?"

"She's going into shock."

Heather snorted. "No doubt, but it's about time Ava got some life into her."

I looked her way. "What does that mean?" I had life in me.

Life. Me.

I was full of life.

Heather must've been watching my face because she only nodded. "Uh huh. Okay." She wiped her hands before standing up. "Okay, this is what we're going to do." She came around to my side, motioning for Bren. "You." She was talking to Bren. "Go back over there."

"What are we doing?" Taz asked as Bren did what she was told.

Heather addressed the other two, "This is what we're going to do."

"I want like five more vodka spritzers."

"Yes." Heather pointed in Taz's direction, but she was looking around. "We'll get those, but this one is a little stunned right now. And since I haven't worked behind the bar, in like years..." She moved me around, guiding me out of the bar area. "You. Go and sit. Bren, come and get her."

Bren nodded, doing as she was told. Again.

Heather pulled out her phone when I got to the stool.

Taz beamed at me before slapping the bottom of my seat. "Pop a squat, our new family member."

"Family member?" I was still in a daze.

"Who are you calling?" Bren was asking Heather.

"I'm calling someone to come and fill in here because this is what we know." She held her hands out, addressing us. "Zeke got into a fight. He told Race that he's in love with Ava—"

I squeaked, another wave of shock coming over me. Shock, but excitement, and then panic, and then—Heather said, "Which is not our place, and we're very sorry that we're the ones who broke that news because it should be a totally private and romantic moment with you and Allen, but I gotta admit that I kinda love the kid. Of course, he'd realize he was in love in the back of a squad car—"

"Squad car?" But wait. Yes. He'd been arrested. "I need to bail him out."

"No."

Heather spoke, but it was Bren who put my phone in front of me. I had no idea where it'd been. I'd thought I had it. Bren said, "He's at the police station, and according to Heather, Godlike Lawyer Logan Kade—"

Heather added, "He got him out."

Bren stopped, but added, relenting, "Okay. Godlike Lawyer Logan *is* taking care of Zeke. We have no idea why Zeke did what he did, but let's all be honest. It's not the first time Zeke's been arrested, and it won't be the last. This is kinda what he does."

Taz shook her head, leaning forward to speak around me, "That's not true, and no offense, Bren, but you don't know the real Zeke. You never have."

Bren was trying for patience here. I was in my whole glaze thing, but even I could tell that.

After a second of silence, Bren added, her voice a little tight, "Okay. Zeke was 'the enemy' when I first met him and through college, he remained an asshole, but I'll admit that he became a likable asshole."

Taz said, "He's different with Blaise, and he's been different for a long time. I've always thought Zeke's been kinda lonely."

My head folded, but I started to look in Taz's direction. She wasn't wrong. He'd admitted something similar to me, and I'd noticed it too. It was what made me start looking at him in a different light.

"Okay. I'll—"

"I like the little dipshit myself," Heather added, putting her phone away. "And we have someone coming to take over for Ava."

I lifted my head up. "Zeke's in love with me."

"You two have been living together and bonking for two months. This is actually surprising to you?"

It was. It really was.

"I think it's great."

I gave Tasmin a small smile.

"Me too." Heather gave me a smile, but hers was wide and

proud. "Now. We need to make as many of those vodka spritzers as we can before Derek gets back."

"You called Derek?"

"Told him it was sort of an emergency. We needed a girls' night. He'll be here in ten."

Ten minutes. The bar was not going to be tended to for ten minutes. That couldn't happen. I started to stand up.

"No!"

"No."

"What are you doing?"

I paused at all of their reactions. "Shock aside, I can still work. I'll make those drinks—"

"No way, you won't." Heather was busy grabbing the vodka and all the mixes. "If I do it, we can claim some ignorance. I don't know what I'm doing, but if you do it, we'll have to pay. Brandon doesn't let his sister get free drinks, so shhh. Sit down. Let me fool around back here, at least for five minutes."

"You make 'em, and we'll squirrel them away in the back."

That was a horrible idea.

Heather brightened up at Tasmin. "That's a great idea!"

Tas beamed back. "I know. That's why I'm here."

Bren sighed.

Heather paused. "We know you're worried. We know you've always felt like you needed to protect Ava, but I've known Ava and in some ways, more than you ever have. If there's anyone tough enough to handle Zeke, it's her. She has been through some extreme stuff, like *extreme* extreme, and you'd never know it. She's tough. Hella smart. Adaptable and she'll outlast us all. That's what I know about Ava. To me, it's no wonder Zeke Allen fell in love with her. He was probably falling for her already back when you went to high school. I wouldn't be shocked. He came in here sometimes by himself and sat in her spot, just so she'd be his waitress."

"He did?" A warmth was spreading inside of me.

"He did. His boy was falling for his own shy girl at the time so who knows, maybe Zeke decided to take a back seat until everyone was okay, also something I wouldn't be shocked about. For whatever reason, he decided to finally make his move. I'm happy for it. Happy for him. Happy for you. As long as he doesn't fuck it up, I think both of you deserve some happy."

I was blinking back tears. The warmth was spooning in my chest, making me smile like an idiot at her.

Taz sniffled. "That was the best speech."

"Thank you."

Taz leaned forward. "But you know what would've made it even better?"

Heather swore. "Gah. You're right. Drinks." She got to work, but eyed Bren as she did. "Sure you don't want one?"

Bren shook her head. "I can't. I—" She stopped herself, cursing under her breath. Her hand had been going to her stomach, and all of us figured out why.

"NO WAY!"

"OMG!" Taz was screaming.

Heather was screaming.

I was smiling and beaming, but still feeling my own happy. Heather ran around, hugging Bren, who cursed again, but nodded. She admitted, "No. I'm sorry. That came out wrong. I'm not pregnant. Just being cautious." She fell quiet, but a little smile came out. "I didn't mean to let it slip that way. We've been trying for another one."

"Either way, I'm still happy. You guys are trying."

They were hugging after that. The drinks got forgotten about, but I'd been pulled out of my own head enough where I could function.

I went back behind the bar and made up the drinks. Taz noticed what I was doing, and after thanking me, she began squirreling them to the back. By the time Derek showed up, I had everything restocked, but slipped enough cash into the till to pay for the drinks.

Heather and Bren had gone to the back. Taz grabbed the last drink and hurried behind them.

Derek stepped around me, frowning. "You okay?"

I nodded. "Yeah. Just life stuff. Thanks for filling in for me."

"No problem, but you're sure that you're okay?"

My phone began ringing at that moment. *Zeke calling.*

I told Derek the truth, taking the call as I did, "Honestly? I've never been better." And phone to my ear, I asked in a rush, "Are you okay?"

19

ZEKE

I wheeled into Manny's parking lot and headed for the bar's back door. Ava told me to pick her up there, and as soon as I parked, she was coming outside, looking all sexy and cute at the same time. Her face was flushed as she climbed in, shutting the door. "Are you okay?"

She was all breathy, asking me, but she'd asked me on the phone earlier.

I leaned over, beckoning for her. "Come here."

She frowned but leaned in. I touched my mouth to hers, and goddamn. Pure sunlight. That's what she was. She hesitated, but after I coaxed her a little, she relaxed into the kiss, and she began tasting me back. I cupped the back of her head, holding her anchored as I took my sweet time saying hello to my girl. I was in love, and the taste was different.

She was like sunlight and rainbows right after a heavy but needed rainstorm. I could breathe her in for the rest of my life. Happiness. She was mine.

She pulled back and fanned herself. "What was that for?"

"Just happy to see you."

She softened, her smile spreading a bit more. "Oh."

I grinned. "Oh." She was hella cute.

Her eyes got serious. "You were arrested?"

My gut tightened up, but I nodded, shifting back and reversing the Jeep. We had an errand to run before heading back to the house. "I was."

"What happened?"

"The guy was saying some shit he shouldn't have been saying."

"What was he saying?"

I was pulling out of the parking lot, turning right, and slid my gaze toward Ava's. "Some shit no man should be saying."

"What's going to happen?"

I was replaying in my head what Logan Kade told me.

"He has an open and shut case. They have witnesses. There was no provocation for what you did, no way you could claim self-defense, so at this point, you either need to get him to change his mind or you find something to bring to offer them instead." He leveled me with a serious look. "You hearing me?"

"Can I scare him?"

"I would highly suggest against that, with this case, this guy."

"If he changes his mind, would they drop the charges?"

"I can't guarantee that, but I can tell you that they are motivated to work with you."

"I'm supposed to narc or something?"

Logan inclined his head, checking his phone. "I wouldn't use that word, but you have connections that their normal confidential informants aren't able to access. You can think on that, otherwise buckle up. If you get a judge who hates privileged wealthy pricks, you could get screwed in the end."

"What would you do? If it were you? If the guy had been saying shit about your woman?"

The phone went down, and Logan Kade set some scary eyes on me. "Then I would already be making calls to find anything on this piece of shit I could, and when I had whatever I needed to bury him,

I'd pay him a visit. I'd make sure he'd be pissing his pants before I left. Course that's contingent on if the DA would drop the charges if the guy wanted them dropped. My advice here? Find something on him to trade for you. And whatever you find, make sure it's something they would salivate for."

I relayed to Ava the gist of what Kade said.

She sat back, frowning. "What are you going to do? Who is this guy?"

"Roger Mitchell."

"Roger Mitchell from my old bank?" She shoved forward, her nostrils flaring.

"I'm taking that you don't like him?"

"He's a piece of shit. You're right when you said that. I stopped using their bank last year *because* of him. Every time I went in, I just felt dirty."

"What'd he do?"

"Every time I'd go in for anything, they'd have to verify through him. He'd come out and handle whatever I needed himself. I hated it. Hated it. The dirty looks. The dirty compliments. I even tried doing the drive-thru, but he stopped that and made it where I'd have to come into the bank every time to either deposit a check or do a cash withdrawal. That's not right. I love my new bank. I'm like a normal customer."

"He did that?"

She nodded. "I thought that was normal since it'd been happening since I was sixteen."

"Sixteen?" I tightened my hold over the steering wheel, imagining it was his neck.

The good news was that if he was doing that, I was sure he was doing other shit. "That's abuse of power. If it came down to it, would you be willing to talk to a lawyer?"

"You think that's enough to get him to drop the charges?"

"No, but it's a start."

She nodded. "Yeah. Of course. I'll do anything you need me to do."

There. Right there. It's another reason I fell for her, and I had plans to tell her. Lots of plans. Elaborate plans, but not yet. We needed to go to battle first. I'd helped with this sort of shit, but it was always someone else's fight. I'd been in the back, helping, supporting. This time, I was at the wheel. It was my fight.

It was time I let people know just what I could do.

20

AVA

We went back to Zeke's house.

"What are you planning on doing?" I asked as we walked inside.

Zeke tossed his keys, went to the fridge, grabbed a beer, and stood, studying me. He took a sip before giving me a grin. "I'm going to hack him."

I raised my eyebrow. "You're what?"

He was nodding, talking to himself now. "Hack him. I bet there's a ton of shit he's hiding. I can get into his accounts. Figure it out and somehow give it to the DA in exchange for them dropping charges against me. Yeah. It could work."

My mouth was on the floor. "What? That sounds like a horrible idea. You could get added charges if you get caught."

"Nah. This will work." He came over, pressing a kiss to my forehead. "This will totally work. This is a great idea." He started down the hallway.

I trailed behind him. "This is a horrible idea." My phone was ringing, but I silenced it. I had a huge catastrophe here to prevent. "Zeke."

He went to the bedroom and started changing clothes.

I perched on the bed, watching, but decided I should change too. He was pulling on comfy clothes, which okay. I loved comfy clothes. Since moving in with Zeke, that was one thing he'd asked us to do more. Or he asked me to do with him, lounging around, wearing pajamas all day, and goofing off. He explained that everyone did it. It was a basic human premise, to be lazy every now and then.

It was now my favorite thing to do, but only with him. With myself, it wasn't the same. I got restless, thinking how much money I could be making if I was working, and ended up heading somewhere to pick up a shift. Thank goodness my bosses all liked when I showed up and didn't turn me away from fear of overtime or something.

But he was pulling on some gym shorts and a T-shirt.

I loved his T-shirts. God. Zeke's chest could be like a Greek statue, and when he was inside me, raised and holding himself over me, his eyes on me, I about died every time. He had tattoos on one shoulder and chest, a tribal one that wound down his right arm, and it was the hottest thing ever to me.

I was getting all hot and bothered, just thinking about it right now, but Zeke wasn't noticing.

He was padding barefoot around the room, nodding to himself. He was all hyped on his world domination plan, or his enemy domination plan. One that I thought was the stupidest plan ever.

I pulled on some lounge pants and a tank top and padded barefoot after him as he was going back to the kitchen. He grabbed another beer, some sports drinks, water, and he filled his arms up with snacks. He gave me a lopsided grin, seeing me standing in the doorway. "You look super sexy right now." He came over, saying, "I need to hack this guy. Save my ass, and then you and me, I'm going to show you the Tour of Europe."

"What?" I almost squeaked, my insides clenching at just what that could be.

He gave my forehead a kiss before dropping to my mouth, and giving me another long and lingering one, one that had me a little short of breath. "Tour of Europe. You'll see. I get inventive."

Okay. Ignoring the sudden pitter-patter in the middle of my chest, I followed him to his office, where he was putting everything around his computer.

I frowned, seeing he was committed to this plan. "Zeke."

He glanced back, frowning right before he turned his computer on. "Yeah, babe?"

Babe.

I'd never been someone's babe. Not even my ex had called me that, but looking at him, my mouth going dry at how good he looked, how earnest he was in breaking the law and seeing no problem in informing me that he was about to do what he was about to do, and now him calling me babe.

I was his babe. I was *his*.

"Did you used to come to Manny's back in high school and sit in my section because it was my section?" I'd forgotten all about those times until Heather brought it up. Now, it was suddenly real important for me to know.

He frowned a little but jerked his head in a nod. "Yeah. I told you that I used to see you too."

I remembered a time in Roussou. "I thought you were laughing at me."

He went still, quieting his voice. "When?"

"When you and Blaise came to the pizza place in Roussou, to pick up a pizza for Aspen. You laughed at me."

"I wasn't laughing at you."

I frowned. "You weren't?"

"I was laughing at Blaise. You asked if he was Aspen's boyfriend, and I thought that was the funniest thing ever because no one asked Blaise random questions like that."

"They didn't?"

"Most were scared of that hothead. I liked that you were asking about Aspen. It made him feel off-balance, just a bit. I wanted you to ask him more questions."

"Right." I was remembering the rest. "He got into a fight."

"Yep." The pride coming from him was...well, that was just Zeke by now. "That's my boy. I miss that piece of hothead shit. Wish he'd decide to play over here in the US." He took a deep breath, sat down behind his desk, and began by pulling up the internet. "The way I see it, you have three choices right now."

"What are they?"

He looked at me, and there was no cockiness, no smart joke, no teasing, no sexual innuendo. Nothing like that. It was just Zeke looking back at me. "I'm going to do this, so you can either pretend you don't know what I'm doing, and I'd suggest heading out for the night so you can claim you didn't know. The second option, call and report me. I know it's wrong, but I'm going to do it anyways."

My mouth was dry again, and my heart was beating hard. "What's the third option?"

"Pull up a chair and keep me company."

I was wrong. It wasn't just Zeke looking at me. It was my Zeke looking at me. Mine.

I was his babe, and he was just mine.

I went over to him and laid a kiss on him. "Kick some ass."

HE WAS adorable when he hacked.

He was quiet the whole time, but hunched over, and squinting. Randomly he'd reach for something to drink or eat, and he kept going. I knew the basics from college. Computers weren't my forte. If I ever decided to pursue a more specialized degree, I'd need to learn, but so far, I enjoyed doing things with my hands. Zeke seemed in a whole different league, and I knew this wasn't the first time I'd thought it. But it was the first time I wasn't scared about it or felt small because of it. I was proud of it. I wasn't proud of what he was doing, but in this day and age, it kinda felt nice knowing he had these skills.

It was scary what people could do in the cyber world.

My phone kept buzzing through the night, so I laid back on his couch and typed back to people.

Tasmin: Checking in on you. You okay?

Me: I'm good. With Zeke.

Tasmin: Good! Back home, and I'm drunk, but had such a good time. You're officially in the fold now. Do you want to do drinks sometime? Or lunch? Or coffee?

This was different. Then again, since Zeke and I became Zeke and I, everything was different.

Me: Lunch would be fun sometime.

Tasmin: Great! I'll reach out later in the week. I wouldn't worry about Zeke. The guys always get into trouble, but they always get themselves out of trouble too.

Me: That helps to hear. Thank you. Have a nice night.

The other person was Bren.

Bren: Hey — sorry if I came across as stern and overbearing. I was just worried, but I know Zeke's a changed guy.

I looked at him, as he was currently breaking the law a few feet away from me, then read the rest of her text.

Bren: I've never seen him in love before. Just, I'm here if you ever need anything. I really am here. I don't usually reach out like this to people so yeah.

And that was major because I knew she didn't. Bren was like me. She didn't have a lot of female friends, or I didn't think she did. Her crew. Her guy. Her family. Her job. That was Bren to me, but I wasn't lying when I texted her back.

Me: I know you care. I've always considered myself lucky to get that from you because I know you're not like that with just anyone. And second, thank you. I really and truly mean it. Having friends is new to me so please excuse me if I'm a bit awkward in this text.

And then there was Heather's text, and I was laughing as I read it.

Heather: I know enough to know that little smart punk is going to do something that'll probably be illegal, but if you need an alibi, I got you. I know people. Also, delete this text after you read it. Also also, I hope we didn't scare you tonight. That's a small preview of the kind of girl squad we can pull in if we need to. You've not even met Mama Malinda officially. She doesn't know about you and Zeke, but when she does, brace yourself. She's a mountain of mama love. Also also also, just know whatever happens, I'm here for you. Channing's here for you. My entire family is here for you. This was true since you were fifteen and first began working at Manny's. Love you lots.

Heather: If you have more 'secrets' for drinks, let me know because you could make a fortune private bartending. I had no idea how killer your drinks are. I'm so proud and rubbing it in Brandon's face right now because he had no clue either.

"You okay?" Zeke asked over his shoulder, not looking away from the computer screen.

I settled back in, knowing I'd respond to Heather tomorrow. "Better than okay. I'm just right."

He glanced back, a small grin on his face, and one that had my chest feeling little flutters.

Oh yes. He was all mine.

I was going to tell him that I loved him tomorrow.

That was my last thought before I fell asleep.

———————————

"I GOT IT!"

I woke to Zeke's cry, and then to his sudden, "Oh shit. Sorry, honey."

I'd been sleeping, and where was I? A couch. I was turned around and looked over my shoulder. He was coming over, his own tired smile on his face. "Hey, babe. I'm sorry to wake you up."

"What's going on?"

I had started to roll over, but he was there and scooping me up in his arms. He lifted me up and started walking out of the office.

"What are—what's going on?"

"Nothing. Everything is perfect. You can go back to sleep."

He carried me into the bedroom, taking and laying me down, and pulling the bedsheets over me. He was tucking me in. "Everything is going to be fine. I've got this. I found the golden goose."

"You did?"

"I did." He gave me another kiss, and then began to pull away. I reached up, grabbed the back of his head. and pulled him back down. His mouth found mine again, and this kiss was more awake. Hungrier.

"I thought you were asleep."

I kicked the covers off me and pulled him over me. "Not anymore."

"Ava." He was hesitating.

I didn't want him to hesitate so I reached up, and moved his pants down, though, God, did I love watching him walk around in those sweats. Seriously defined muscles, and sometimes he wore a gold chain. I reached for it, finding it around his neck. He must've put it on when he was hacking. I used it and pulled his mouth to mine. He'd told me once that it'd been a gift his dad once gave him. It was a sort of initiation when he graduated from Cain University. He didn't always wear it, but I was glad he was wearing it tonight.

I wanted. I needed. I was in control here.

"Ava."

"Shut up." I scissor-kicked him so he was on the bed, and I was up, above him.

I sat down, straddling him, finding him right where I needed him. And at the touch, I paused, just once, before I moved over him. He groaned, his hands finding my hips. He began kneading me there, but he was sitting up, finding my mouth.

He battled for control, the way I'd known he would. He liked going rough, which I liked too, but there'd been some times when he went slow. Tender. I didn't want that, and I could feel the build-up in him. He was riled up from the hacking. So was I. I was riled up for him, and I was fully fucking awake and dripping for him.

I began moving harder over him, a hand planted on his chest.

He moved with me, urging me down, as his mouth opened over mine, his tongue slipping in.

This man. He'd been a boy when I'd first met him. A bully. Mean. Then he changed. He became a man, and now he was my man and I was breathless from needing him. From yearning for him. Another emotion was rising up in me, curling around my spine, and I felt it building. It was making me breathless all over again, but I opened my hips and sank farther down on him, and tried to clamp that feeling from bursting out of me.

Not yet.

He rolled me over, rising up over me, and I stretched, savoring from this viewpoint too. I loved watching as Zeke held himself above me, watching me, catching my chin, and holding me in place so I could feel him looking into me. It was like he was reading into my soul, seeing beyond every wall I had, every thought that was in place, every hesitation, and he blasted through them. Because he could. Because he was Zeke.

My Zeke.

He leaned down, his mouth touching mine in the softest kiss, and he asked, a whisper against my skin, "I'm going to make love to you tonight."

Yes, yes. Please yes, and I let all that out of me in a soft sigh as his mouth moved down my throat, down my body. My shirt was lifted up and over me, and his mouth was on my stomach. He kept going, searching, exploring. My shorts were pulled off. My thong was next, and he was kissing me there, holding me in place as I screamed, then I was erupting. And still he took his time, his hands moving over my body, then sliding under me, lifting me up as he moved back over me.

He paused at my entrance, his eyes finding mine. We held each other's gaze and I reached for him, cupping the side of his face, before I lifted up and kissed him. As I did, he slid inside of me, and I sighed, "Yes."

He groaned, his forehead finding my shoulder. He held still before lifting his head again, finding me. He was waiting for me to give him the go-ahead. I grinned because I fucking loved when he did that. I reached up, grabbed a hold of his gold chain, and I pulled on it as I slammed my hips against his.

That was my go-ahead.

He began thrusting, and I stretched out, riding with him.

I WOKE UP TO DARKNESS.

It was all black. The ceiling fan was working, and I looked over. Zeke was next to me, his chest rising up and down steadily.

I remembered what he had said earlier. He found the golden goose.

Everything was going to be fine.

He called me honey.

I was a honey and a babe.

My stomach was just melting all over again.

I slipped out of the bed, headed for the bathroom, and officially got ready for bed. When I was done, I snuck back out, and crawled into bed.

He rolled over, his head buried into his pillow, and his hand found my hip. "You okay?"

I nodded before saying, "Yeah. Bathroom."

His fingers squeezed me a little before he began caressing me, rubbing his hand up and down over my hip. "Ava."

I stilled. "What?" I reached for him too, finding his chest and I began rubbing him in the same manner. He sighed, his entire body settled under my touch.

He said it, so quietly, "I love you."

I paused, my whole body paused. Had I heard him right?

I lifted my head up. "What?" I wanted him to say it again. I wanted to hear it again.

He pulled me over to him, hugging me to him. "I love you."

"Zeke." My hand spread out, and I was feeling the hot and steady rhythm of his heart. I waited... I was going to tell him back.

His snores told me I'd have to wait.

I let out a soft sigh but relaxed over him and he hugged me even more to him in his sleep.

I loved this too. Cuddling. It was something new to me. I'd never cuddled with anyone before, but now, I just let myself collapse on top of him.

It felt like the most natural thing in the world to do.

I fell back asleep too.

21

ZEKE

I was on top of the world, or that's how I felt. Ava was still sleeping when I eased out of bed, so I considered it a success that I didn't wake her up. I left my gold chain with her. She'd enjoyed holding onto it last night. My plans for the day were to kick ass, grab some coffee, and go back and make love to my lady. I was in my Jeep and heading out to cross off number one. I was halfway to Banker Mitchell's house when my phone rang.

Blaise calling.

I never hesitated on answering my dude's call, but I was hesitating now. But fuck. He was calling at this time because he'd heard something. If I didn't answer, he'd keep calling and he'd sound the alarm so everyone would be calling. That was just how my boy operated.

I hit the button. "Early for a call."

Blaise swore. "I have access to your doorbell camera. You forget that?"

Shit. I had.

"Where are you going at five your time?"

I made a face, one that he wouldn't see and one that I wasn't proud of, but that's how I was feeling right now. "Dude—"

"Dude, don't! Talk to me before you do something stupid. I can't fly back to bail you out, and after getting a call from my sister, I know that you're going to do something stupid."

"I have to do this."

"Does your dad know? Did he call you?"

"He doesn't know yet, but he will. And yes, he'll call, but I'm going to have this handled by then."

He cursed on his end. "Talk me through it first."

"That'd make you an accomplice."

He swore again. "Zeke, I swear. Cut me in. Tell me what you're doing."

"You know what went down?"

"I heard you swung on Banker Mitchell. Taz informed me he's known to be a perv among the female population. Knowing you, hearing about him, I'm guessing he was saying some shit about someone you care about. Ava?"

I relaxed, just slightly. My boy was smart. I always liked that about him. "Yeah."

"You swung, with witnesses, and let me guess? You're backed into a corner unless you force your way out somewhere."

"Pretty much, yeah."

"Logan's your lawyer?"

"Your phone must've been burning up today."

He grunted. "The voice messages, yeah. Can Kade get a lower sentence? A plea deal at all?"

"I'm not doing a plea."

"You could be charged on assault—"

"I hacked him."

He was quiet. "You did what?"

"I hacked him."

"Banker Mitchell?"

"Perv Mitchell."

He was quiet again. "You're going public with your skills?"

I had to grin. "I'm a late bloomer and my rep is firmly that I'm a dumb jock, well; now I'm sure it's probably that I'm a has-been. You're not a has-been, though. You're a pro-fes-sional athlete. Yes, you are." I was almost singing the last five words.

"You're stalling so I can't talk you out of doing whatever you're going to do. Stop. Pull over. Talk me through it. Come on, Zeke. I'm usually your partner in crime."

"You're across the ocean."

"Yeah, well, I won't always be over here. Talk. To. Me. You told me a long time ago that you needed guys to look up to so you wouldn't become the guy you were becoming. That's when your dad was working all the time and not around. Me and Kade. You aspired to be like Mason, and I was the only guy who'd stand against you. You said you needed that. Consider this the same fucking shit. Talk to me."

I tightened my hold on the wheel. "I don't want to stop. If I do, I might not go through with it."

"That's a flag right there. Whatever you're going to do, *think*. If it goes wrong, what's the worst thing that could happen?"

"Extra criminal charges on me."

"Okay. Let's focus on that. Look, I'm not saying don't go through with it. I mean, fuck. You know I've done some seri-ously shady shit in the past."

"Shit I helped you with."

"Yes. Shit you helped me with, so the situation is reversed. I want to help you, but I can't help you unless you *tell me what you're doing*."

I checked the time, and I had ten minutes. Only ten. I pulled over but let the engine idle. "I got a small opening. I need to get to him, get in place, when he's alone."

"What are you going to do?"

I set a timer and told him.

22

AVA

My phone was waking me up, ringing over and over again, and I couldn't understand why Zeke wasn't shutting it off. He always did if I got a call. I'd roll over as he would hand me the phone. I'd either take the call or not, but in both situations, he'd want me to stay so I'd flip to my back and answer while he would pull me in closer and settle in more firmly at my side.

None of that was happening.

I woke enough to look around. No Zeke.

My phone kept going, so I grabbed it and answered without looking at the screen. "Hello?"

"Ava?"

I frowned, looking at the number. "Who is this?"

"This is Aspen. Blaise's—"

Holy shit!

I sat upright, panicked but controlled panic clicking in immediately. "Where is he?"

She was quiet, for just a moment. "Okay. That was fast." If she was calling me, it wasn't good.

"Where is he?" I repeated.

"Blaise is on the phone with him right now. He just left your place. We know where—"

I threw the bedsheets back, grabbed a robe, my purse, and I was running out the door. "Where?" I nabbed my keys on the way, going into the garage. Zeke tended to park outside, which I had no idea why because he had a four-car stall garage, but he had insisted I use the first slot.

I reversed as soon as the garage door lifted.

"He's heading to Roger Mitchell's house."

I was disgusted, just on principle.

And I must've made a sound because she asked, "You know him?"

"He's disgusting, but yes. I know where his house is too. My ex used to drive his wife home. I'm pretty sure he still does." My ex had been the local Uber driver. I'd been along a couple times back then, and I couldn't imagine Mitchell moving. The house was massive. So I swung in that direction.

Zeke would've taken the main highway, but there was a short cut around. I could maybe get there first.

"Blaise is making him wait and tell him what he's planning."

That was all I needed to hear. "I'll try and get there first."

"Okay. Good luck. Also, it's super cool that you're coming into the mix."

That made me smile. "Thanks."

"We can talk later, but it'd be awesome if you and Zeke could come over sometime. I know Blaise really misses him."

She was right. That would be awesome.

But first, I pressed my foot down on the accelerator.

23

ZEKE

He liked to swim in the mornings, and he swam alone. They had their own pool, set back, in a building all by itself. I parked behind their wooded lot and made my way over their land. The door wasn't even locked, which made my task easier.

He was in the pool, swimming, with his head down. Front crawl. He had goggles. A hair cap. He wore a speedo, so as he kept swimming because according to his schedule, he had five more minutes to go, I went about getting everything ready.

The doors were locked.

The windows were shut.

I made sure the security cameras were off, or when he'd look back, he'd see they had been paused. No alarm.

He had the side wall pulled back with the screen still shielding against animals, bugs, but I moved to start sliding that closed. I had moved to a back chair before he stopped, resting a bit at the end, before heaving himself up and to the edge. He sat there, feet and legs still in the pool and taking deep breaths, his head slightly folded over his stomach. Then, as if deciding it was time to go, he swung his head up and back, climbing the rest of the way.

He was padding halfway to the table where his towels were before he noticed the side wall had been closed. His hand closing around one of the towels, he began looking around, and he started to wrap it around his waist, the ends not quite together when alarm finally settled over him. He jerked around, seeing that each window was closed. The smaller doors were as well.

He sucked in his breath, and I knew what he was looking for as he began twisting around, his eyes not lifting up enough to see me. He was scanning the tables set around the pool.

I was sitting in a chair, far corner, in the shadowed area of the building, and I leaned forward.

He heard the squeaking of the chair and froze. His gaze went right to me, but he frowned because he couldn't quite see who I was.

"Who are you?"

"You don't recognize me? My feelings are hurt." I half laughed, sighing at the end because it wasn't funny. Not at all.

"Allen?" He scowled, starting to stomp around to where I was, one hand holding his towel together. "I'll have you—"

I raised his phone up and pressed play.

Moans filled the room, echoing.

He paused, his head rearing back. "You're really messed up. Playing porn for me—"

His own groan sounded next. "Yeah, yeah. Do that, baby. Turn over. Let me see you—"

And *her* groan.

He had frozen by now.

Not me. I turned that recording off and played another.

His own voice came out, "Benny, my man. How are you? Listen, I need you to—"

He growled to me, "What the fuck is this? What are you doing?"

I smirked, though he couldn't see me. "Don't you want to hear what you ask the chief of police to do for you? Or don't you need to hear it to remember?" I smiled. "Because I know what you asked him to do. I don't need the reminder."

"What the fuck are you doing, Allen? You need to tread real carefully here because you're a pup playing among—"

"Shut up." I said it casually because that's how I was feeling. He wasn't getting it. I played another.

"Felicia, I need you to call me. This isn't a smart thing you're doing, not returning my calls—" That one I ended because he didn't seem capable of talking.

I rose from the chair, holding his phone up. "These were recordings I found on your cloud. They were recordings you kept. One of you on a sexting call with another woman. Another where you asked an officer of the law to look the other way when your boy got caught with drugs. The last one, where you blackmailed one of your employees into sleeping with you. These alone will land you in a pile of trouble."

The blood was draining from his face, but me, I was starting to have fun.

"I found these the first ten minutes."

His eyes narrowed. "Wha—"

"Can you imagine what I found after three hours?" I stepped forward, letting him see just how much fun I was having.

He didn't respond. He didn't seem capable of standing anymore either.

"I found enough where I could send a nice file, all put together with a pretty bow on top, to the FBI and they'd be interested in it. You have companies in other states. Fraud. More recordings. More blackmail. Recordings of conversations you've had with other people, other very powerful people. I've no doubt you were keeping those as evidence that you'd have against others, not thinking if they fell into the wrong hands how it'd look for you to have them."

"You are way out of your league, little boy."

"Maybe. And you're probably right because I just showed my hand, that I'm capable of getting all this information on you, whereas you're the one who has such dirty and bloody hands. Am I right?" I chuckled. "I know I'm right. I've done shit, but you're right. I'm in no league that you are, but this is what I'm going to tell you that I do have. I have access. I have skills to get access even when you try to hide it all again, because we both know you will. What else do I have? I have connections. Granted, they aren't my connections, but it wouldn't take much to reach out. There's a motorcycle club not far from here, and I know they have ties to people I know. It wouldn't be hard to put the word out, asking for a meet and I think they'd take it. I think they'd be interested in a deal where you withheld money that was owed to them. Course, that's in the past so maybe they're the forgiving kind? Between you and me, I doubt it. And what else do I have? I have people across the ocean who are aware of this very conversation happening, so if you get the bright idea to try and graduate from the shithole you're in to, say, a more murderous shithole, well, there's witnesses listening in." I pulled my phone out and let him see that it was active and someone else was there.

He stared long and hard at me. "What do you want?"

"First, I want you to call your bud Benny and tell him to drop the charges against me."

"He won't—"

"Be persuasive," I cut him off, going through his phone and hitting play on another recording.

The chief of police's voice played from it, "Goddammit. That kid is bleeding us dry. Plant shit on him, if need be. I want him gone. Do you hear me?"

"But Ben—"

I was smirking again. "We know what the rest of that said, and I know what the rest of the recording said, but I bet the kid he's talking about would be very interested in hearing it. Should I send it? He's probably out of prison by now."

He was gritting his teeth. "You've made yourself more than heard. I'll call and get your charges dropped."

"Great!" I beamed at him before tossing a third phone his way. "Do it now."

He frowned, catching it, and staring in confusion at the phone. "This is—"

"Yeah. That's your phone too." I raised the one I was holding, the one that was also his. "This is a clone of your phone, and by the way, good luck figuring out how to de-clone it. Also, just letting you know that if you try to get a new phone, everything you have on there will be transferred to your new one, including the cloning program. The only way you can start new is a new phone and all new accounts. Which you won't do because that's exhausting. Am I right?"

"That's too much evidence you have on me."

"You're right. It is, and I get that. So, here's what I'll do: as soon as you get the charges dropped against me, I'll turn the cloning program off. I'll even show you how I do it."

He was looking between his phone and the one in my hand, his eyebrows pinched together. "I don't get it. There has to be a catch."

"There's no catch. I'm going to be honest, when I decided to hack you, I had no idea what I would find. I figured there'd be *some* things there, but not the landfill I found. I'm only here for two reasons, to make you drop the charges against me and to let you know that if you think about coming after me, everything I found was sent to five other people. So, if something happens to me, they'll release the information, and I'm talking about anything, like an accident. Or if I end up in a coma, anything

like that where I can't tell them that you weren't behind it.
They'll make the assumption that it's from your hands. I have
no plans on getting into a pissing contest with you. That's not
who I am. I'm usually a go-with-the-flow kind of guy. My
friends, not so much, but we can't all be blessed with my
amazing genes. So, are we good? Have you pissed your speedo
enough?"

He looked visibly shaken. "Be careful, Allen. I still do business with your father."

My grin was gone. "Yeah. The very few recordings you had
on him, where you blackmailed him, those are gone. You'll
never find them again. Don't enter into a pissing contest with
me. You're an artifact when it comes to technology. In that
world, I'm the giant and you know it." I nodded at his phone.
"Make the call, Mitchell."

He did.

There was protesting on the other end, but he got him to
drop the charges, saying he recently rethought about pissing off
Allen Sr. The chief agreed about a bit, telling him that my
lawyer would be notified within the hour.

Once he was done, I showed him the cloning program and
hit the stop button.

He was searching his own phone for where it was, unin-
stalling it immediately.

I didn't have the heart to tell him that actually activated the
secondary one I had planted because that'd been the plan.
With guys like Mitchell, I figured I might want to keep an eye
out on what he was going to be doing in the next few weeks,
just to be safe.

"Your girlfriend still has an account at my bank. She doesn't
use it, but it's still there."

I had started to leave, feeling there wasn't anything else to
say. I was corrected and I spun around, my old smirk back in
place. "No. I closed it for her this morning. All records you have

on her are wiped." I gave him a two-finger salute, heading for the back door.

"Zeke," he called after me.

I didn't turn around but paused with the door half open.

He said, "Be careful. I'm a small bee in a larger hive."

I gave a small nod because I was fully aware of it. There was always corruption that I could hack. This time, it was my first time doing it for something like this. Guess we all had to grow up at some point.

I waited until I was off his land, back in my Jeep, before I spoke to the person on the phone.

"Did you get all that?"

Logan Kade said back, "I did, and I concur. I had no idea what I'd be listening in on when I answered your call, especially fascinated that you told him someone had been listening the whole time since I only caught the last ten minutes. You're full of surprises lately, Allen."

"He had a murderous look to him. I was thinking on my feet."

"I gathered, and I'm guessing the call I'm getting from the Fallen Crest Police Department will be the Chief letting me know your charges have been dropped. Would you like me to reciprocate and you listen in as well?"

I was starting to laugh and agree right as someone got inside my Jeep, on the passenger side and slammed the door shut. "Uh. I better not."

"Zeke—"

I hung up. "What are you doing here?"

24

AVA

"Y
ou're blackmailing people?"

I was furious. And trembling. And my God, I couldn't stop shaking so I sat on my hands. But I kept glaring because that was really important. Glaring. Letting him see how enraged I was, and my word, I—I didn't know what else I was feeling because it was all rolling together in my tummy, in one molten ball of lava.

His eyebrows shot up. "How do you—" Wariness came over him. "Aspen?"

"Yes, Aspen. She called me and told me what you were going to do."

He cursed, looking away.

"Are you kidding me? Do you know how much trouble you're going to get into for this?"

He looked back, his eyebrows furrowing together. "I'm not, that's the point."

"Zeke—"

"No, Ava. Listen. This is what we do, in my group of people. We blackmail and we burn buildings down and we fight people and we break into places—it's what we do."

"I don't!"

I couldn't. No, no, no. I had too much to lose.

My grandmum—my mom. I couldn't lose my mom. I tasted salt and flicked away whatever tear had trailed down because it wasn't helpful right now.

"You don't get it."

"I do!" I cried out, because I did. I really did. "You think that people don't watch you? That they don't see what you and your friends do? And I know you're all connected. You to Blaise. Blaise to Aspen. Aspen to her brother. Her brother to the Kades. The Kades to my boss! My boss to Bren and her whole group. You're all interconnected and I *do* know what you guys do. I just thought—" I looked away because what had I thought? That Zeke was different?

He wasn't.

I was the fool for thinking that.

"You and people like you don't understand that when you guys do the things you just said, you're not the one who gets hurt. For whatever reason, it's not you. It's never you. It's the others. The bystanders. The people on the outskirts. It's people like my mom, like my grandmum. It's people like me." My voice cracked. "We're the ones who get hurt and we're the ones who have to spend the rest of our lives dealing with it, surviving it, existing despite it. My grandmother couldn't escape my grandfather. She kept expecting him to come and 'finish her off.' That's how he was, how she was. That kind of thing doesn't leave you. It stayed with her, stayed with my mom, stayed with me. My mom lost her legs in an accident. Did I tell you how she lost them?" I turned away, tasting my tears, but my God, he needed to understand it. "My dad was drunk, and he got into a fight. And he was driving, and my mom was in the car, and guess what happened? She lost her legs, and then *he* left *her*, so she lost her husband too."

He looked visibly stricken. "Ava—"

"She lied." I just kept tasting those tears. I guess they needed to be released. "When the cops came in and asked what happened, because my dad was sober by then, she lied. She said he lost control. It was raining and it was just an accident. He repaid her kindness by leaving her because he didn't want to be saddled taking care of a disabled wife. Those were his words. But if you ask me, she's not disabled. She's not anything. She's my mom, and she's never let her not having two legs stop her from doing a damned thing. It never will. If she's gotta get upstairs, trust and believe, she will. She will lift herself all the way up, two stairs at a time, and she'll rig a rope or something and get her chair up behind her. My mom can do anything." My voice cracked again. "But I can't. She's the survivor, not me. I'm exhausted. That's what I am. I am just exhausted from life because the whole of it, I've just been trying to get by while the rest of you, the God-blessed ones, you *live*. Not me, though. Not me." I knew I was fully crying, and I didn't care.

I was just feeling the crushing weight of the impending doom coming my way. This time, I knew I wouldn't outlast it.

I loved him. That gave him the power to destroy me. The kind of destruction that I wouldn't survive.

I was shaking my head before I knew what I was going to say, what I *had* to do. "I can't do this, Zeke. Maybe it's me. I can't handle it again. I can't stand by and... I don't even know what *will* happen, but something will happen. To me or to you, and I can't deal with it. I'm not made of that tough stuff people seem to need to thrive in the world. I don't have it, and what's worse, I don't know if I want it. If I have to blackmail someone or break into someone's house or set someone's car on fire—I don't have that in me to hurt another person. Whether they're good or bad, or if they deserve it or not. I just don't have it. Consider me weak, if that's how you perceive it. I just don't have it in me, that's all I know."

"Ava," he spoke, softly.

That made it hurt, but I was already hurting. I'd be hurting for a long time. I knew that, but this way, I can still stand. I wouldn't be able to stand whenever my world would shatter, and this was my life. Of course, it'd shatter.

I was getting out before it happened. It's the only way I could survive this.

I'd run out of words and there didn't seem to be anything else to say. I'd made up my mind except, I looked at him. "I can't do this with you. I'm sorry." I left, sliding out of the Jeep and somehow, I made it to my own vehicle.

I drove away, not having a destination in mind.

I just needed to go away.

25

AVA

I went to my mom's place, and she opened the door, wheeling back and stared up at me.

I shrugged. "What? You've never seen me wrecked before?"

She only pressed her lips together before jerking her head. "Come in. And I'm not saying this to be a mean mama, because I'll always have time for my daughter, but I'm getting picked up for movie night tonight." She motioned with her wrist. "Let's hurry this along."

I grunted, rolling my eyes, but went to the kitchen table and sat.

She zoomed in, going to the fridge and grabbing a beer for both of us before closing the door, and grabbing a bowl of popcorn she already had on the counter. She came back, hitting one lock on her chair before handing the beer over. The bowl went on the table between us. "Okay. I'm here for you, daughter of mine." She patted my arm before opening her beer and tipping it back for a sip. "Spill. What'd your new man do?"

I gave her a look. "You don't have to sound so brisk about this."

She gave me a look right back. "I love you, but your

grandma left us both explicit directions that we're supposed to live life to the fullest. I'm living and you're living, and you're really living. Got a hot new and well-off man, but you're here moping. You're moping at my kitchen table. I know you enough to know something happened with your man. Let's hear it out. Tell me. Come on." She made a waving motion with her hands before grabbing some popcorn.

She really was hurrying this along, and I gave her a whole different onceover.

Her hair was freshly cut, and cleaned, and shining. There was gel in it, giving it extra volume. She had makeup. Not a lot, but a little, enough to give her some extra shine there too. And she was wearing a skirt, along with a white frilly top.

I shoved back my chair, gaping at her. "You have a date."

She looked away, scratching the back of her neck before she grabbed more popcorn. "I do not."

"You do too. You're dressed up."

"I am no—"

"You have makeup on!" I pointed at it. "And lipstick. You have *lipstick* on."

"I—"

"You said it's a movie night. Is this a group thing?"

"Yes. There will be a bunch of people there."

"That means you like someone in the group. Who do you like?"

"Oh—stop it, Ava. Tell me what happened between you and Zeke—"

"Who is it?"

"Sweethear—"

"Tell me who it is, and I'll tell you what happened with Zeke."

She opened her mouth, gaping at me, before sighing and cursing under her breath. She reached for another sip of her beer. "Sophie."

"Sophi—" I knew Sophie. She was a friend of one of the other ladies in the building. "Sophie's a woman, Mom."

She grunted. "I'm well aware, and I like her." She was eyeing me. She was really eyeing me. "I like her a lot, Ava."

I held her gaze, and I was quiet for a beat because this was something major. Like uber super-duper major. My mom had never expressed that she was attracted to a woman before. Then again, my mom had never expressed she was interested or attracted to anyone, not even my father now that I was thinking about it. Except Charlie Hunnam. We both shared our delight in him from *Sons of Anarchy*.

"Mom—" I started, going gentle.

She cursed, wheeling back and staring at me head on. "I like Sophie. That's it. Since you showed up, I felt it was time to tell you. That's all I want to say about it."

"Okay, but—"

"Ava!"

"Mom." I laid my hand over her arm because this *was* important. This was suddenly so extremely and very important and I needed her to hear me say my part.

She stilled but cursed and looked away.

She was two seconds away from letting a tear come out. I knew my mom. I knew the signs.

"I need you to hear me. Just in case you need to hear this. I will always love you—"

"Oh, good God. I know you'll always love me." But her voice was a little shaky, and she reached for my hand, entwining our fingers. "Thank you." She squeezed my hand again. "Thank you."

I sat there, and there was a whole burst of emotions going on in me.

I had no clue what to do here because this wasn't about me. This was about her, so... well, screw it. I was going with what felt right to say.

"Mom."

She groaned. "Ava. Stop. It's—it's fine. You can leave it alone."

"I love you, Mom."

She looked away but tipped her head up. That meant she was listening to me, listening to every word I was going to say.

"You're my mother. I feel weird saying "I still love you' because that means that something might've happened where I might not love you and that'll *never* happen. Ever. So instead, I'm going to say that I have always loved you. I have always needed you. I have always depended on you, and *nothing* will change that. Nothing. The main thing I care about right now is that I want to know how long you've liked her? Because if you've had a crush developing on her, I'm a little pissed that I didn't figure it out before you told me."

She was smiling and those tears were still there, but she shook her head. "How'd I luck out getting you as a daughter?"

"Lucked out? What are you talking about?" I asked softly right back, smiling tenderly. "You're the one who raised me, Mama. I'm all you."

She kept smiling and kept blinking her eyes at the same time. "Are you going to tell me what happened between you and Zeke?"

"I'd like to know more about you and Sophie."

She barked out a laugh, before shaking her head. "I don't know about me and Sophie. I know I like her. I know she makes me smile. I know I want to hold her hand, and I know I want to kiss her. That's what I know. That's all I know right now. Your turn. What's going on with you and Zeke?"

Oh, boy.

I let out a soft sigh because in a way, it was the same. Except, "I'm in love with him."

"Oh, honey." She leaned in, cupping the side of my face. "Why are you saying that like it's a bad thing?"

Because he blackmailed someone.

Because I knew he'd do worse if he needed to.

And because no matter what he was doing, I still loved him.

"Because my heart's going to get ripped out by him one day."

"How do you know?"

I held her gaze, her hand still holding the side of my face. "Because I'm like you. We don't like unless we're going to love, and we don't love unless it's forever." I smiled at her, while I felt my heart being ripped apart. "And because the forever tends to never happen for us. That's what I know."

I gave her a sad smile. "How much hurt can we take?"

"Oh, Ava. Honey." She wheeled all the way in, locking both sides, and reached for me. She cupped each side of my face, and she looked right at me. Eye to eye. Intense. "I don't know what he's done to bring this on, or if he's done anything. Maybe you're just running blind, but no matter you're the only one that can judge that. If he did something, can you understand why he did it? It's only until you understand what he did or why he did it before you can make a decision moving forward."

Her words cut through me because I didn't know why he did what he did. I never asked.

"And if he didn't do anything? If I'm just running blind?"

Her hand fell to mine, and she squeezed lightly. "Then it's time you stopped running because I can see how much he loves you. I can see how much you love him, and isn't it worth a try?"

"What's worth a try?"

"A try at being happy? Isn't it worth it?"

26

AVA

I was waiting on the golf course when Zeke arrived. I'd been sitting down but stood when he got closer, frowning at me and carrying what I'd asked him to bring. He held it up. "Why'd you want me to bring this beer?"

My palms were sweating. I wiped them over my shirt, nodding to the bottle in his hand. "That's the beer you were drinking the night I accidentally walked here?"

His face was closed off, but he nodded again. "Why'd you want me to bring this again?"

"Because." I reached for it, opened it, and took a sip before passing it back to him. "That was the night I thought everything was ending. Do you remember?"

He kept watching me, his eyes narrowed, but said, "Yes."

"Well. I liked the beer. I never told you, but I think that's my favorite beer."

"Okay." His head cocked back. There was a slight softening around his eyes, but his mouth was still firm. "What are we doing here, Ava?"

"We—" I was so nervous. I gestured down. "Can you sit? Can we sit?"

He looked around, but it was after dark. The course was supposed to be closed, and I had called to make sure there wouldn't be a late-night party. "You like to golf."

He snorted, but sat and leaned back, stretching his legs out. "I golf. I don't know if I like it. It's one of those sports you grow up doing and you have to keep doing because everyone in your world does it. I like drinking when I golf. I do like that."

I nodded, my stomach still doing somersaults. "Right. That's good." I looked around because I thought I had all of this planned. It wasn't going how I thought it would go. Then again, I'd never done something like this before.

"Ava."

I paused and looked over. He'd said my name so softly. "Yeah?"

"What are we doing here?"

"I'm trying to do a new leaf thing. And I'm trying to apologize for earlier." I held his gaze. "For what I said, especially at the end."

"That was this morning."

"I know."

"Where were you all day? You didn't go to any of your jobs."

I frowned. "How do you know?"

"Because I scoped them out, all day. You never showed, and they wouldn't tell me anything."

"Oh." A nervous laugh slipped out of me. I started rocking, self-soothing. "I called in to the stables, said I needed a self-care day. Then I went and had lunch with my mom and she, well, she changed my mind about everything."

"Everything?"

I nodded, a firm one. "Everything."

He tilted his head to see me better, and I was beginning to feel warm from the look in his gaze. They were knowing, somber, but also kind. He was giving me the look he'd done when he saw me walking drunk here and when he took me to his place, and when he gave me food, and when he held my hand after my grandmum died, and all the other times that I hadn't branded to my memory. I was doing that now.

"I overreacted—"

"No, you didn't."

I paused.

He leaned forward, his head still turned my way and I realized that Zeke never looked away from me. He always had his eyes on me. Steadfast. "I poked a bear this morning, and I might have to keep poking it to make sure it doesn't poke me back. You don't know the reason, but—"

"I don't need to," I rushed in, cutting him off and my hand laid on his arm. "I don't need to know the reason you did what you did. I don't even know all the details, just that you went to someone's house, someone that I loathe, and you blackmailed him with something you found when you hacked him. It's a whole different level for me, but you're a different level."

"Ava." He began to shake his head. "If you start on this where I'm here, and you're here, and we're too different, or if you start talking about the differences in our socioeconomic status, I'm going to hurl this beer bottle off into the dark. And I know you hate that shit, so you'd have to go and look for it, and then I'd have to go with you because it's dark out and who knows what creatures are scurrying around here, and I don't want to do that. You think I'm all this brave guy, but I'm really just a scaredy cat."

I was fighting back a grin. "You'd be going to protect me?"

"No. I'd be going so you could protect me." His tone was dry, and he was giving me a subtle look. A subtle hint. The ghost of a smile was on his face, just briefly. "I told you, I'm the scaredy cat here."

"But you're not." My tone went serious. "You *are* the brave one. You're the one who wades into any battle that's going on if it means helping out one of your friends. I don't know why you swung on Mitchell, but I can take a guess."

I was holding his gaze this time. I leaned in closer, dropping my voice. "When I thought about it, I figured that probably Dirty Mean Mitchell said some not-nice things, probably about me, maybe about others, but most definitely it was bad enough where you reacted."

"I'd do it again."

My heart thumped, real hard in my chest. "I know you deleted my account with his bank. Someone I know who works there called me this afternoon. She was worried, heard what happened, and knew about you and me. She looked me up, saw I wasn't there, and panicked."

"Your money is safe. I just transferred it all to your other account. I was going to tell you, but shit hit the fan."

"I won't lie. It's alarming that you can do that, what you did."

"I was only protecting you."

"I know." I moved up and touched a hand to his chest, moving him back so I could sit on his lap. I liked getting up close. One of his hands went to my leg, anchoring me in place. "I know all of that. I know why you did it. I'm just saying that's a little scary, but—" I held up a hand when he started to say something. "—I realized today that I have somewhat hid from life. I think. I hid in work. I hid in my family. I hid when I didn't go to graduate school. I even hid in my ex. Remember Jarrod?"

His hand curled around me. "The offer to beat him up still stands. I don't think I scared him enough."

I smiled a little at that. "In the grand scheme of things, Jarrod was no one to me. I hid in him because problems my parents were having, and then I hid in Roy because Roy was everything Jarrod wasn't. Roy was a good guy. Kind. Nice. Not flashy. Not charismatic. Roy was like me. He was steady."

"Not enjoying hearing about the either ex. It makes me want to do something stupid, again." He gave a low growl.

I held up a hand. "I'm getting to my point. Roy worked all the time, but now, looking back, I think he was hiding too. He was like me in that way. Then he met someone, and he fell head over heels for her. I didn't understand. I was okay with it, but I just didn't understand." I tipped my head back to get a better look at him, moving so I was straddling him. Both of his hands moved to my back, one slid down to my ass, palming me. The warmth just kept getting warmer inside of me. "Until you."

"Me?"

"Until I fell in love with you."

His whole face softened, and the corner of his mouth lifted. "You love me?"

I nodded, so serious. "You scare me. You unnerve me. You challenge me. You are the opposite of me in so many ways. And you make me live. You make me smile. You make me laugh. You make me feel loved, and that scares me, but Zeke, there is no one like you. No one will ever be like you. You are the foundation that supports others, and you are a foundation for yourself. You don't need anyone to stand for you, and I don't think you even realize that about yourself. You've not asked anyone to stand for you, but I will. I want to. I want to be the one who helps you stand at times."

"Babe."

"I started thinking about all the firsts I've had with you. My first beer. The first time someone broke into my apartment and crashed my pity party in the bathtub."

"Speaking of, we should do that again. Tub sex is fun."

I grinned but felt all the tenderness swelling up inside of me for him. "The first house party where it was where I was living. My first time watching someone hack. My first time finding out someone I knew had blackmailed someone else *for* me, to protect me." I leaned in until my forehead was resting against his. "The truth is that you terrify me. You are so full of life, and you come in and that whole world is at your beck and call. You are larger than life sometimes, and there I was, hiding from life and you blew everything away until it was just me. Just you. And somehow, in the middle of all of that, I fell in love with you and that made me even more terrified, but you know what's worse?"

His eyes were so tender. He lifted a hand and ran the side of his knuckle down my face, real gentle. "What?"

"That now that I've had you, I can't not have you. You've ruined me. You gave me sunshine when I didn't know I needed it, and now all I want is your sunshine. You can't take it back, even if I'm the reason. You can't do that. That's what terrifies me the most now. Losing you."

"Babe," he whispered, his forehead resting against mine. "You're sorely underestimating me. I'm like cling wrap. Once I care, you'd need to murder me to get me to let you go. I consider it my superhuman trait. I'm not going anywhere."

I shuddered in his arms, and he shifted us so I was even closer to him. He ran his hands up and down my back, going to my hips and holding me in place. "Something else where you and I are different was today. You thought we broke up, and to me, I just heard you asking for some space. I gave you an hour before I started looking for you, and look at me. I was waiting for you to call and either yell at me, or I don't know. I was just waiting for you, because no matter how I get your attention, it's *all* like sunshine to me. You being here. You texting me. You getting mad at me. You yelling at me. I'm okay with it because it's you. You're my fuzzy dandelion."

"What?"

"A fuzzy dandelion. You know those flowers. They're fuzzy and you blow on them to grant you a wish. That's you. You're my wish."

I couldn't. Laughter bubbled up inside of me. "They're a weed and they're so hard to get rid of."

"Then maybe I'm your fuzzy dandelion. I like them the most when they're fuzzy. They're the wish granters. The yellow ones are pretty too. You can be the yellow dandelions, my sunshine in a flower, and I'll be the fuzzy ones. See. We're not so different. We're perfect for each other. We're the same flower."

He was grinning so wide, thinking he was so smart.

"The same weed?"

"I'm the weed. You're the flower."

I shook my head because he was getting it wrong. He was the flower right with me. And I could just imagine all the dandelions he'd find for me from now on, but I'd love it. I let out a soft sigh and settled back against him. "I love you."

He got all serious. "I love you too. But do me a favor?"

"What?"

"I am predicting that we're going to have a long future of times where you're going to get mad at me because I've done something stupid because I just do that at times. You're going to call on the girls, and they're going to swoop you up and you might even declare you're done with men. But if you do that, remember that I'm your dandelion. Pretty to look at it, but always there. And when you calm down and start missing your fuzzy dandelion, you call me, and I'll come running. I'm not going anywhere, but also, don't take this in a scary way because I'm a *dandelion*. I'm not a stalker. I'm thinking about the words I'm using and want to clarify that. Weed. Not stalker."

"The wish flower. Got it." I fought back my own laugh. "This is the time when you can shut up and kiss me."

His whole body sagged in relief. "Ava, I'm wishing you'll let me kiss you for the rest of your life."

I leaned forward and my mouth found his.

IT WAS WAY LATER when the thought came to me, and why it hadn't before? I'd never know.

"You hacked Jarrod, didn't you?"

His arms tightened around me. We were in bed. "I might've."

"Simple cyberstalking, my ass."

He chuckled, but moved in closer to me, nuzzling the back of my throat. "Anything for you, Ava. I was already falling for you."

I laced our fingers. "Love you."

He brushed a kiss against my forehead. "Always, Ava. Always."

EPILOGUE

AVA

We were at the Fallen Crest Bingo Hall a few weeks later, and why we were there? Because Zeke picked it for our date night. We'd started a routine since he liked to say that we were somewhat married, since we lived together, and since the whole living together was totally working out. It was great. Almost unnervingly so.

Zeke was Zeke. He was happy. Supportive. Loving. Loyal. And sweet. So very sweet and romantic, and I didn't know how to handle it sometimes when he laid out fresh dandelions next to my morning coffee and that was on mornings when I had an early shift at the stables. So yeah. Things were going well, but Zeke insisted we have "date nights." He'd said, "We need to keep it fresh and spicy," and because he had read on an online marriage and therapy website that scheduling regular dates helped "to get away," he had decided that was what we needed.

"It never hurts to start great routines. Habit, baby. Our dates will be routine and a part of what we need to keep sane in this cycle we call life. You pick two and I'll pick two."

This was Zeke's pick tonight. Fallen Crest Bingo Hall.

When we'd first walked in, Zeke stopped and grinned at me. "Please tell me you didn't work here back in the day?"

I laughed but shook my head. "No. Though, I did volunteer here one time and never again."

He raised his eyebrows.

"Let's just say they can be ruthless here."

Now he frowned.

We were set up toward the back of the room, both of us with three cards in front of us. Zeke made sure we were on the end, but he wouldn't tell me why. He just kept laughing, almost giggling to himself. A lady surrounded herself with crystals in front of us. Another had trolls to the left of us. And behind us, a guy had thirty gnomes set up on the end of his table. All had stone cold sober expressions. They meant business. Then there was a table of teenagers on the other side of the aisle, all giggling and being hushed by the others. And a table of college students not far from them. I didn't think they were together since one group refused to look at the other. Plus, the high schoolers had Fallen Crest Public letterman jackets while the other table had a couple people wearing Cain University apparel. I didn't know what they were doing in Fallen Crest, but they were here.

Zeke's phone lit up, and his smile stretched as he took it. "Kade."

I could hear a low murmur on the other end.

Zeke leaned back, resting his arm over the back of my chair, and kicked his legs out in front of him. One ankle crossed the other. "We're in the back. Go in and aim right. You'll see us behind the Crystal Lady."

His phone went dark, and he put it in his pocket before glancing my way.

He was planning something. He could barely hold back his glee. I raised an eyebrow. "What are you doing?"

"Nothing." But his lips pressed together, and he was trying to hold back laughter.

"Zeke." I looked around but didn't see anyone coming our way. "Who's coming in here? Kade?"

"You'll see." His shoulders were almost shaking.

I knew about the Kades. Mason and Logan Kade. One needed to, well, *not* live in Fallen Crest to not know about them, so everyone knew about Mason and Logan Kade. Two brothers who ruled their school and this town. And Samantha Strattan, who moved in with them and fell in love with Mason. The stories were long and probably dramatized over the years, but they were legends. Samantha was best friends with my boss and was still tight with Heather, so yeah, I knew them. Knew *of* them, knew them, it was somewhat the same deal for me because I kept out of their proximity. I was on the outskirts and had no interest wading in. They operated on a whole different level than I ever wanted to be a part of. They were powerful, but with power came danger and both Kade brothers were known to be dangerous. And from their best friends, who were connected to Blaise, who was connected to Zeke, I considered Zeke "in there" with them. But thinking *that*, I didn't think he was so close to the actual Kades themselves so I wasn't too worried. But then Logan Kade took Zeke's case when he was arrested...

I thought that'd been it. Zeke had his "man/mentor" crush on Mason Kade, but to my knowledge, Mason Kade didn't want much to do with Zeke. That was an answered prayer to me, but now, hearing a Kade was coming here and seeing how excited Zeke was, my tummy was knotting up.

A second later, Logan Kade walked inside, scowling, and wearing shades. He wore a white dress shirt and dark pants. It looked like he left his business suit jacket in his vehicle. His dark hair was messily rumpled like he'd run his hand through it a few extra times. He had a firm scowl on his face, over his square jaw, and as he paused behind the tables, sweeping over them, he unbuttoned his shirt and began rolling the ends up until he could push them almost to his elbow.

Spotting us, that scowl just deepened as he made his way toward us. "Allen." His gaze went to me and softened. "Ava."

I held up a hand, my stomach one big knot by now. "Hi, Mr. Kade." See, I knew them, knew of them, and it was the same from all the times they'd come to Manny's, but I never considered seeing them in a social way.

At my greeting, Logan's head jerked while Zeke barked out laughing.

He gave Zeke a look. "Shut it unless you no longer need legal counsel from me."

Zeke turned away, but he didn't "shut it." He kept laughing, just quieter as he moved his head down.

Logan sighed, pulling a chair out across from us. He opened his mouth to say something, but an attendant came over. "Do you want bingo cards?"

"Uh."

Zeke stopped laughing enough to straighten back up, and coughed, nodding. "Yes. He'll take five cards."

"Five?" came from Logan at the same time the attendant nodded and said, "Yes, sir." And he ran off.

Logan leaned forward, shoving his shades up to rest on top of his head. His brown eyes were not happy. "This isn't a social call, Allen. I'm in town and you said you had something to discuss with me." But the attendant was back and placing the cards in front of Logan. He cursed, leaning back so the attendant had more room.

"I did." Zeke's lips were still twitching. "Bingo."

Cursing again, Logan cut his gaze my way. "I heard you hitched yourself to this guy but was hoping it was a joke. I'm seeing that Jax wasn't just imagining things."

Zeke's lips stopped twitching. His tone quickly went low.

"You can be a jackass to me. I get it. I take that shit and it slides off my back, but don't disrespect Ava. She's tenfold the person you and I both are. Keep that in mind."

Logan's eyes cleared, his mouth turned down, but he was softening again. "Sorry. I didn't mean that in a rude way. Just surprised. I thought you were with–"

Zeke lowered his head and focused on his bingo cards, but his words still came out, sounding casual, "Would you like me to start asking about your woman's exes? I'm sure Taylor has a few." Yes. His voice sounded carefree, almost cherry, but he glanced up and even I got a zing from the hard look in his eyes. He held Logan's gaze for a full beat.

Logan's shoulders rose up, held, and then lowered.

B10 was called out.

Logan began looking over his cards, placing tokens on two of them. "Oh, my God. I'm actually playing bingo. What is it you wanted to talk to me about, Allen?" His eyebrows shot up. "And if you called me here to play bingo with you, I will put you on the holiday blacklist because you and I both know you're hoping to get an invite to Christmas."

"You have a point, but..." Zeke stood up, and reverted to his almost giggling self. "One second. I'll be right back."

Logan frowned before saying, "He's like a lovable gnat, and no offense because his crush on my brother sometimes alarms both Mason and me."

I sat up straighter. "No offense back to you, but do you actually know him?"

He got quiet but held my gaze.

I added, "He could've gone down a much different path. That's how he was growing up and he changed himself, decided he wanted better mentors. He did that. No one else."

Logan cocked his head to the side. "I heard he got a nice push from his best friend and his father."

"And your brother. You talk about him like he's a fanboy.

You're wrong. He chose Mason to look up to, to help him into being a better guy. The idea of your brother, but he's the one who made that decision to look for a guide. He's the one who latched onto Blaise. He's the one who didn't get pissed off when his dad did what he did. The way I heard it, Zeke lapped it up and he used that to make himself a better person. Takes some intelligence and discipline to make the decision and then follow through with it."

"Yeah. You're right." A different look edged into his gaze. "Other guys like Zeke might've gone a different way." Those eyes were suddenly all-seeing, and I saw the sharp intelligence in them, a ruthlessness there that gave all those stories told about him some credibility. "Just as long as he treats you right."

I frowned.

Logan smirked. "Heather loves you. Adores you. And because she does, so do we. You just didn't know that part."

My frown deepened. Zeke had made reference to something like this. I knew about Heather, Brandon, my other bosses, but to hear those words being said from Logan Kade? Who *I* knew, but I had no idea he knew who I was.

I couldn't react. I didn't know how.

Logan laughed a little. "Heather said you're kinda clueless about how much you're cared about. See she's right."

"You don't even know me."

"You've been serving me food and drinks since you were fifteen." He leaned forward, his voice gentling again. "You're seen. And if Zeke wasn't attached to you, I wouldn't have taken him on as a client."

I snorted at that. "I know that's not true."

He looked ready to argue.

I got there first. "It's Zeke. He would've hounded you, and you know it."

He growled. "I don't like to think I would've given in under said houndage."

Now my grin gentled. "It's Zeke."

He nodded, giving in. "You're right, and–oh my fucking–" He shot up from his seat and pointed. "Take that out of here. Now. I don't want to see that."

Zeke was carrying a six-foot cardboard cutout of Mason Kade in his NFL football uniform, a football tucked under his arm. He had his helmet on and was staring hard at the camera. Zeke positioned it at the end of our table, and I was now understanding why he insisted on getting seats at the edge. His chest was puffed up as he took his seat.

"I mean it, Allen. I'm not going to play bingo with you staring at my brother's cardboard cutout."

"G,15."

Zeke was still laughing, but he saw he had G,15. He motioned to Logan's cards. "You better look to see if you have it because they're not going to call it again."

Logan was glaring at him, still standing.

"I,7."

Zeke covered his. "Oh!"

Logan groaned but was eyeing the cards before him and cursing. He scrambled to cover two more of his cards. "Shit. I almost have a bingo."

We kept playing, and Logan did in fact get a bingo. He also kept asking Zeke to remove his brother's cardboard cutout, but Zeke just ignored him every time. When they announced we needed new cards, it was an hour later. Zeke had taken to holding my hand under the table, and Logan was the one who got up to get us all new cards. His phone kept ringing while we were there, so Nate Monson, another from that group, was going to join us. When Logan was gone, I leaned over. "What's with the cutout?"

Zeke grinned, his finger rubbing over the inside of my palm. "Consider it my good-luck charm."

I shot him a look. "Zeke."

He laughed again. "Don't give it away, but I actually ordered two. The other one is inside of Logan's Escalade. He'll find out when he leaves." Kade came back after, and Monson was with him. Both sat down, and we played for another two hours.

ZEKE NEVER HAD anything to talk to Logan about. He was told he was in town and made the call, but it was when we were heading home that I brought it up. "You owe me another date night. That didn't count."

He was holding my hand – he always reached for me when he could – and he lifted our hands to kiss the back of mine. "I know. You pick the date tomorrow night."

"I work the closing shift at Manny's tomorrow."

"We can do something after or the next night you have free? I'm easy either way."

He was. We did midnight golfing the next night.

IT WAS another night after Manny's when I walked into the house and saw a giant bouquet of dandelions on the counter alongside a cardboard cutout of myself.

"Zeke!"

He came in from the hallway, holding a box in his hands. "You like them?"

I pointed at myself. "What the–"

"Oh yeah. That."

"Yes! That. What is that doing here?"

He went over and put his arm around it, smiling wide at me. "I only get cutouts of the people I look up to." He was teasing, but then he got serious. His eyes got dark, and he came toward me. "Jokes aside, you're the only cardboard cutout I want in my life."

"What happened to the Mason Kade one?"

He shrugged. "The bingo people asked if I'd leave it with them."

I started laughing, and kept laughing even as he lifted his hands, cupping the side of my face. "Like a mascot?"

"Probably." His thumbs swept over my cheeks, and I noticed the box he was still holding. It was cupped into his palm, resting against my face.

"What is this?"

He was suddenly really serious.

My heart dipped. "Zeke?"

"Okay." He seemed flustered now before bringing the box between us. It was a jewelry box. Velvet.

A lump rested on the back of my throat. "What is this, Zeke?"

"It's not an engagement ring." He said that quickly and rushed. "I mean, shit. I should've put this in a different box. I'm not trying to be an asshole, in case you thought it was an engagement ring and now I'm saying it's not, but..." He stopped talking, trailing off as I reached up and took the box from him. He stepped back, his head lowered. His shoulders hunched down, and he shoved his hands in his pockets.

It was a pendant on a chain.

My heart began beating so fast as I lifted it out of the box.

"It's—" His voice grew thick. "It's a single dandelion wish. A seed. And they preserved it in the glass. I found it online when I wanted to get you something special." He moved in close again, so close I could feel his heat. I was still staring at the dandelion as his forehead slowly lowered to rest on mine. His hands went to my arms and his thumbs began rubbing over me, soft, tender. "The store's website said it's to be a token. To remind you to always keep working toward your wishes and your dreams. And I got it for you because you're my wish."

I lifted my gaze to his and saw how he was staring at the pendant in my hand.

He added, his voice hoarse, "I said it before, but I wanted my person when I was growing up. I just never had that person... until you. You're my person, Ava. My wish. My dream. No one else was it because it was always you. I love you." His eyes went to mine, and my heart melted at the vulnerable look on his face.

"Zeke," I whispered, reaching up and cradling his face. "You're mine too."

So much love pounded through my whole body. It heated up my chest, sent my blood coursing, and I was going on another memory binge because this wasn't the first time that Zeke had done something nice like this for me, and I knew it wouldn't be the last. Simple things like bringing me food at the stables. Making coffee for me in the morning. He was always kind and thoughtful, and the complete opposite of what he used to be known as.

We had a monthly bingo night with my mom and Sophie now, and he always liked to get Logan to join if he was in town. Blaise FaceTimed in to play his own card a few times when it worked with his schedule. And Zeke tended to need sugar when he did stocks so I always made sure to bring home his favorite: gummy bears. And he liked doing couple massages and going to the spa. He also enjoyed going to sporting events, so for his birthday, he was going to get tickets to the Arizona Javalina, Mason Kade's football team, and the Kansas City Mustangs.

"And I'm pre-proposing to you now."

"What?"

His face was solemn. "We've not hit a year yet. I know you're the cautious type, and moving in with me was a big deal for you. I know that so I'm respecting that, but just so you know, I'd marry you tomorrow if you said you wanted it."

I took a step back. "What?" My stomach was now in my chest. "What are you saying?"

He was studying me, his eyes widening. "Oh–I didn't mean it to scare you. I'm trying–fuck it. I'm trying to be thoughtful. I know girls like these things." He held up the jewelry box. "So if you were hoping this was an engagement ring, and then you found it wasn't, I'm trying to cover all my bases here. I didn't think you'd want me to propose so soon, so I'm pre-proposing... if that makes sense?"

I couldn't breathe. Not for a second, but I managed to choke out, "It makes no sense."

His face fell. "Oh."

I continued to whisper. "You'd marry me tomorrow?"

His eyes held mine. "After our first fight, I told you I wished to kiss you for the rest of my life. I would've married you that day. The day after. Today. Tomorrow. I'll marry you any day you want, and all the days after. You say it–"

"Yes."

My heart skipped a beat.

He frowned a little. "What?"

Was I doing this? Yes. I knew it so assuredly, so strongly. I never knew anything with more certainty. "I want to marry you too."

His eyebrows shot up. "I–when? Where?"

"Now. Here. I don't care. Vegas."

"Are you serious?"

I jerked my head in a nod. "I'm serious."

He came in, his hands cupping my face. "I don't think I've ever loved you more than right now. I mean, I'll love you more tomorrow because it's growing every day, but I love you. A lot, *a lot*. Right now. I–"

"Zeke."

"What?"

"Shut up and kiss me."

His mouth found mine, and the earth moved, and we kept kissing.

––––––––––––

WE FLEW to Vegas the next day, after I got time off from both my jobs, but we also had another ceremony the next summer in Fallen Crest. Blaise was Zeke's best man. My mother was my matron of honor. We had a large party at Manny's, then another at our house, and yet another at Fallen Crest Country Club. (Zeke knew the board members.) His family was there. Sophie was also there, and she had her own ring by then as well.

A certain cardboard cutout also made the bridal party. I'm not going to say which one.

There was a bachelorette party thrown for me by Heather, Tasmin, Aspen, Bren, Taylor, Samantha, Quincey, and so many others. Zeke had his own party too, and yes, Mason Kade showed up for it. Zeke was over the moon, but I knew the main two guys he really wanted there were his father and Blaise. My other bosses from the horse stable also threw a party for me, and they had a different group of friends celebrating us, but I knew them and loved them as well. All in all, it was a whole party extravaganza and so much not me, but it was me now.

It was me because besides loving Zeke, I'd let so many others in and this was what it was like to find your happily ever after. It wasn't just the guy. It was yourself. It was accepting and welcoming love, and I was glowing.

And three months later I had another reason to glow.

I was pregnant. I was half considering ordering a baby cardboard cutout to give to Zeke when I told him.

I hope you enjoyed Aveke!
If you did, please leave a review.
They truly help so much.
For more stories, go to www.tijansbooks.com

Read Blaise and Aspen's book here.
Read Bren and Cross's book here.

ACKNOWLEDGMENTS

I wrote the first 10k of this book as a short story for an anthology. Then, later on, I expanded the rest so it's actually a very large novella. Because of that, I want to thank Zeke and Ava both for helping me write their stories. I knew bits and pieces of both as I wrote the Crew series, The Boy I Grew Up, and Rich Prick, but sometimes the characters don't really show me their lives until I write their stories. And having written Aveke, I love love love both Zeke and Ava. There's such a quiet courage and humbleness to Ava, and Zeke, I just love how he doesn't care how he comes across. He's true first and foremost to those he love.

Thank you to my readers because you guys have really helped me with so much support. Thank you to Crystal, Amy. Serena. Tami. Eileen. Kay! To everyone who proofread this one. I really and truly appreciate all the help you give me.

And as always, thank you to my Bailey. I love that little guy so much.

RICH PRICK

1

Everyone knew who Blaise DeVroe was.

It didn't matter that he'd come to Fallen Crest Academy late in the year—and FCA was *not* a school you showed up late to.

I knew this because I showed up shortly after this year—my senior year—began, and no one, I repeat *no one*, knew who I was. Since my parents decided to have a mid-life crisis and tried to make up for some of their wrongs and bring me back to Fallen Crest, my last year of high school had sucked. FCA was filled with rich, stuck-up people. That meant you had to speak their language to be in their groups, and I didn't. Not because I didn't have money. My parents were movie producers and directors. We had money, and I previously went to one of the most exclusive private schools in North America, *and* a stint in a boarding school in Europe.

I could be fluent in stuck-up-ese if I wanted to.

But I chose not to. I've never been that girl.

I was the library girl.

I was the book nerd girl.

I was the wallflower.

On the whole, I tended to avoid people. I didn't people well.

I had an affinity for blending into the background. It's a skill. I'd been perfecting it all my life.

But anyway, Blaise DeVroe was the opposite of that.

He may have moved to this school late in the year, but he walked in as if he already owned it. And to his credit, he kinda did.

The guy who ran the school before Blaise showed up was Zeke Allen. He's this wealthy jackass who's a bully, a muscular douchebag, and who slept with girls and then talked shit about them. He was king of the school by default, I guess—not because he was anything fantastic.

Then Blaise DeVroe walked in.

Guess who gave him a welcome-home hug? Zeke Allen did!

I was there, just coming out of the counselor's office, so I saw it all.

Blaise DeVroe strutted in with that cocky walk all the athletes had, and he was gorgeous. Like, seriously gorgeous. He had the high, arching cheekbones only the prettiest of the pretty-boy models had.

I knew this too because I'd done some reluctant gigs in the business.

But back to freaking stunning Blaise DeVroe. He had a chiseled, square jaw. He could have had his own waterfall off that jawline. Dark eyes. His hair was short, but long enough so he could rake his hands through it and let it be all adorably messy. And his body. Don't even get me started on his body—I was all crushing on it because it was *sick* and I mean that in the hot kind of sick way, not the real sick way. He was definitely not the real sick way at all.

He wasn't as big as Zeke, but he had these big, broad shoulders. Trim waist. And there were muscles everywhere. I swear I saw shape definition in his neck.

Blaise DeVroe: the *hottest* guy at Fallen Crest Academy.

One of the richest guys too.

I didn't hear the story of why he came here—not the real reason. Rumors circulated that his mom was going through a divorce, but there were also whispers about secret siblings. I wasn't on the up-and-up with anyone, so I never heard for sure if any of that was true. All I knew was Blaise DeVroe had walked into the hallowed and pretentious hallways of the private school in our town, and he was hailed like a long-lost son or something.

Or something, as it turned out.

Blaise and Zeke knew each other from childhood. Zeke considered him his long-lost best friend. So it was a coming home sort of situation.

Not that I could talk much about the history of FCA, because I was new myself, but I had been here almost a whole semester before Blaise. And full disclosure, I'd been here when I was much younger at the private elementary/middle school. That was before Mom and Pops decided they didn't like the influence my older brother's best friend was having on him, so they pulled both my brothers and me out of here.

But that's a whole different story.

The story for right now is that I'm being a total weirdo stalker and perving on Blaise DeVroe getting his dick sucked.

Like, right in front of me.

In hindsight, this was probably not the best idea I'd ever had. And I've had some doozy ideas. But this one takes the cake. I just couldn't help myself. As I've mentioned, I usually keep to myself, but something got into me this year. Every time I heard about a party, I couldn't make myself go, but I also couldn't *not* go.

So...I went.

But I stayed on the outskirts, so the people actually attending the party didn't realize I was there. There'd been a big bonfire that our town and the neighboring two towns had a while back. I was there, but I'd decided to make it a camping trip—just for me.

I was there, but not there. And that night had ended weird too, but nothing like this one.

This time the party was at Zeke Allen's lake cabin. Not that his cabin was a cabin. It was a mansion—a twenty-room *mega* log cabin, which no one even blinked at, because that's just normal for these people. Most everyone was staying at the cabin, not trekking back here into the woods like me. I'd set up my tent a bit away, doing my camping thing again (something I love, by the way), when I heard voices. They weren't down by the house, spilling out over the back patio, or even at the lake. Nope. These voices were up the hill, coming from farther into the woods.

I'd done my research. Zeke Allen's cabin was set a good ten miles away from the nearest neighbors. I should've been in the clear to sneak onto their land, do a little freestyle camping, and listen to the party sounds like the loser I was. But noooo. I was about to get company.

As I snuck out of my tent, and realized who it was, I almost crapped my pants.

It was Blaise DeVroe, holding hands with Mara Daniels.

As popular girls went, Mara Daniels was one of the nicer ones. She was on the dance team. Dark hair. Shorter, but athletic. The problem with Mara was that she was friends with the other popular girls. Some of them were nasty—hence the reason I wasn't friends with them. Not that they'd tried to get to know me. Not that I even registered on their radar. But then again, that's what I did.

I didn't engage. I didn't attend. I was on the edge. I was the invisible girl, and here I was, being the invisible girl once more, but man...

When I saw it was him, and then saw how his hand went from holding hers and guiding her to a tree to slipping around and grabbing her ass, something came over me. I couldn't retreat back to my tent. I couldn't even stay hidden behind a tree and just listen.

I know, I know. This was all sorts of wrong, but Blaise was Blaise.

He'd become the guy in my dreams, my weird schoolgirl fantasies. He was my high school crush. Everyone had one. If you didn't, you're even weirder than me, and that's saying something. So when I started salivating over Blaise DeVroe, I kinda just let myself go. I mean, nothing was ever going to happen. Guys like him didn't date girls like me. They didn't even notice girls like me.

I wasn't crazy. That'd make me all sorts of delusional.

I was a realist. I knew my place in life's hierarchy. I was at the bottom. I was not the very bottom—because of my family— but socially, I was barely one rung up the ladder.

Anyway, when Blaise started kissing Mara, when Mara knelt in front of him, when she opened his pants and took out his cock—I lost all train of thought.

I watched as she took his dick in her mouth, as her head began bobbing up and down over him.

And, oh my God.

My whole body was awash with sensations, and I was captivated. Captivated! Entranced. Mesmerized.

I could not look away.

Then I felt throbbing and a warm feeling between my legs, and it was game over. It was all I could do not to make a sound, because I wanted to. So bad. I wanted to moan. I wanted to touch myself, but I didn't. I kept myself reined in, but watch? Oh yeah. I watched.

I couldn't *not* watch.

I watched the whole thing.

I loved the whole thing.

And then at the end of it, I almost died.

BLAISE

I was getting my dick sucked while a weird chick watched us.

"Hmmm...Blaise." My girl moaned, readjusted, and took me in again. She reached up to stroke under, and damn, that felt good. My eyes almost rolled back, but I caught myself and held steady. My hands went to her head. Sometimes a little guidance went a long way, and as I applied gentle pressure, my girl was receptive. So I started to drive her mouth over me. All the while, I never stopped watching the other girl.

I couldn't place her.

I was pretty sure she hadn't been at Zeke's party, but who the fuck knew. He'd invited fifty people, way more than he needed to, but Zeke was a lovable bully idiot. He was mean. Some might say he had a slime effect on them, but he was my best friend. I couldn't judge. I had an attitude the size of fucking Alaska. Anyway, back to Zeke. He liked to go big, and that included his parties and his fuck-ups, and there were a lot of both.

That girl...

I liked her.

Fresh face. I could tell she was light on the makeup. Her face was one of those that would look jaded under a ton of crap, but without it, she looked the way she did right now: innocent and pure. Though the fact that she was watching my blowjob didn't fit either of those adjectives. She was tugging on her lip now, her hand lingering on her shorts.

Christ.

Her shorts.

My chick was wearing a bikini top and shredded jean shorts —and those shorts were hardly there. They were more decorative so she didn't get arrested for public indecency. All the girls at this party were like that. Bikinis, and anything else they wore was painted on their bodies. The old school way of thought might've labeled them sluts or whores, but since we were all liberal and progressive, we went with *sexually healthy appetites.*

I, currently, was enjoying my girl's appetite.

She opened her mouth wider, angled her head to the other side, and oooh yeah—I was in at a whole different depth now. Fuck it. I took hold of her hair and started moving. She moaned, but only widened her jaw and spread her knees a little more apart. She was bracing herself.

Fuuuuck yeah.

That meant I could go a little harder, which I did. I shoved her down a bit more, a better angle, and right there. I loved when they let me take over. But then I looked back up to watch Voyeur Girl. My friends and I did not hang out with girls like my voyeur. My dick got harder. I almost cursed, gritting my teeth. I had not expected that reaction, but I'd take it.

The girl watching wore a buttoned-up maroon shirt, the ends tied at her waist. She had a good rack. The shirt was bunched up to hide 'em, but I saw her girls. They would be a decent handful, almost perfect. And she wasn't wearing a bra. There was enough of a tease between the buttons that I could see just skin, just tits.

The rest of her... I had no words.

Khaki shorts that ended mid-thigh, and what a fucking thigh she had.

This girl could model.

Long. Lean. Legs meant to wrap around your waist—I thrust a little harder, and my girl groaned around me. I needed to ease up, but I was almost gone. Almost. Not quite.

Then Mara reached up and massaged my boys. That was enough.

I unloaded into her.

She swallowed like a champ and smiled up at me. She

wiped her mouth with the back of her hand, and for a second, the weird chick was forgotten. I grinned at Mara. I always liked Mara's blowjobs, and because I wasn't an asshole, I tugged her up and moved her farther behind the trees so she was hidden from view.

Now was my turn to make her feel good.

Kissing her, I slid my hand inside her shorts and inside her, and when she was done and moaning, I looked over my shoulder. The other girl was still there, still glued to her tree, her eyes still right on us, but this time, she saw me.

Her eyes bulged out, and she inhaled sharply. She jerked back, and I grinned, lifting my hand to my mouth. I tasted Mara on my fingers as I watched her. Then I winked.

She uttered a muffled scream.

Chuckling, I grabbed Mara as she tensed in my arms.

Her head snapped around. "What was that?"

"Nothing." I kept her tight to my side as she fixed her pants. "Come on. Let's go back to the party."

As we left, I glanced back.

The girl was gone.

Read the rest here!

THE NOT-OUTCAST

1

I was lit, weak, and horny.

That was not a good combination for me. Usually my willpower was strong, like industrial-strength super-latexed condom strong, but not tonight. Tonight, the combination of the booze and cocktails had melded together and taken down my last holdouts of willpower. I was gonzo and then I got this text.

Dean: Mustang party! Now! Where r u???

Dean was my colleague, but let's forget about why he would be texting me because we are not 'texting' colleagues. Kansas City Mustangs. That was the important part of that text, and it was getting all of my attention.

Dear God. I could hear the whistle of the impending bomb right before it hit.

That was the professional hockey team that *he* played on.

Party.

Did I mention the *he* that was him? He, as in the only rookie drafted for Kansas City's newer team? He signed his contract after he had one year at Silvard.

The *he* that the team's owners were hoping could be grown into one of the NHL's newest stars, but that'd been a three-year plan. Nope. *He* had different ideas because once he hit the ice in their first debut game, he scored a hat trick in the first period. First. Period. Playing against five to ten-year veterans, and that had not gone unnoticed. By everyone. After that *he* exploded into the NHL scene and in a big fucking way.

They started calling him Reaper Ryder after that.

It was the same *he* that I perved on during a brief stint in high school, and then again during that one year in college before he got whisked away to superstardom. Though, he didn't know any of that 411 about my perving habits.

The second text from Dean gave us the address where to go, and the whistle got louder, target hit...direct implosion.

It was two blocks away.

He was two blocks away, and there went my restraint because I'd kept away from him for the last four years when I moved to the same city he was living in—of course he didn't know that—but this city was totally amazeballs by the way.

I was doomed. I might as well start digging my own bunker at this rate because I was already downtown partaking in some celebratory boozetails, so here we were. Here I was, well *we* because I wasn't alone. My main girl since Silvard days, Sasha, was on my right, and Melanie on my left. Melanie came after Silvard, but that didn't matter. She was one of my girls. The three of us. We were awesomesauce, and we were walking into this building that looked like a downtown loft, one that was probably the humble abode to someone not so humble, but someone with old-money wealth who enjoyed partaking in their own boozetails as well.

I already felt a whole kemosabe camaraderie with whoever owned this joint.

"This place is *fucking* awesome."

That was Melanie. She enjoyed coffee, girls, and she was an

amazing barista at Dino's Beans.

"Girl."

That was Sasha. She owned a strip club, told everyone she was an angry Russian, even though there wasn't one Russian strand of DNA in her body, and she enjoyed using one word for everything. That's not to say she didn't speak more than one-word answers, but those were her go-to for speaking.

"Whoa." That was me.

Melanie had jet-black hair. Sasha had ice-queen white hair, and me—I was the in between. My hair was usually a dusty blonde color, but today it looked a bit more lighter than dusty blonde. I still enjoyed it, and I also had super chill electric-blue eyes. The other two both had dark eyes so I figured I was still the 'in between' for the eyes, too.

When we entered that party, all eyes turned to us, and not one of us was fazed. We were used to it. Where we went, we got attention. Guys loved us (sometimes), girls hated us (usually), and we didn't care (ever). We weren't going to tone down our awesomeness because of their insecurities.

But we were all works in progress, or at least I was.

I was known to have entire conversations and whole other worlds and every version of apocalypses in my head. That was just me. You'll understand the more you get to know me, but trust me when I say that I'm a lot better than I used to be. Meds, therapy, and a dead junkie mother will do that to you.

But enough about me.

Melanie was the shit, and she really loved the word 'fuck.' A-*fucking*-lot.

Then there was Sasha, she'd been my roommate from college, and here we were, three years out of graduation (well, four for me since I graduated early, and don't ask me how that happened because it still shocked the hell out of me) and going strong. But we were on a mission.

That mission was more boozetails.

There were people everywhere. Stuffy people. One woman who had a tiara on her head. There were guys in suits, some in hella expensive suits, and tuxedos, too.

Whoa.

This wasn't just a party party. This was like a whole shindig party.

Fake Stanley Cups were placed all around with mucho dinero inside.

Crap.

I started to mentally shift through the emails—easier said than done when one was halfway to boozeopolis—that I liked to avoid and I was remembering some of the subject lines of those that I had skipped. There'd been a bunch from Dean lately, though, and one was about some 'Celebrity PR for Come Our Way' and I needed to double down on the crapattitude because I had a feeling we just waltzed into a fundraiser.

"Cheyenne!"

Dean rushed over to us, holding a boozetail in one hand, and his eyes glazed over. He was medium height with a more squat build that he easily could buff up more, but I didn't think Dean went to the gym. He was always at work and because of that, I usually saw him with his hair all messed up. That's how it was now, and his eyes glazed over.

My dude coworker was lit.

I started smiling, but then no. Not good. What corporate espionage was he up to by telling me to come here?

"Where's the bar, Deano?" Melanie.

I was impressed she hadn't used her favorite word.

"There." Directions from Sasha and like that, both my buds moved away.

I settled back, knowing they'd have my back. They'd be bringing the boozetails to me—even better—so I had the time to grin at Dean. "What's happening, hot stuff?"

He never got my quotes. Or jokes.

He didn't react and he grabbed my arm. "Have you read my emails?" Then he looked at me, his head moving back an inch. "What are you wearing?"

Nothing appropriate for a work event, that's for sure.

But I only upped my grin wattage. "I was going for a Daenerys theme. Felt like wanting to tame some dragons tonight." Except I took my own liberty with the outfit. Instead of her flowing robes and dresses, I was wearing a leather, almost corset-like top, one that wrapped around my neck and hung off one of my shoulders. The bottom was more Daenerys theme, a chiffon skirt with a slit up one thigh. And high heels strapped to my feet.

It shouldn't work, but it did. It so totally did, and I had woven colored threads in my hair so they were swinging free, free and lit.

He took another step back, looking me up and down again.

"You are," a pause, "something."

I scowled. "Dude. Insulting."

He had to blink a few times because he hadn't realized I spoke again, then he refocused. "Wait. You're downtown. There's no way you could've gotten here this fast, even if you were at the shelter, but I know you weren't at the shelter. And your place is an hour out."

Case in point, my outfit.

He was right.

Come Our Way. The name of our kitchen had been a marketing and genius ploy, one put in place by Deano himself, because while I wrote the grant that got us five million (not a common thing to happen for a start-up) and got us going, his job was actually to work on marketing and promotions to keep the money, spotlight, and volunteers streaming to our little kitchen. I maintained our grant, and I helped with literally everything else. I was the final say-so on all executive decisions, except for matters that we needed the board to oversee. We had another full-time staff member, but she liked to Netflix and chill (and really Netflix and chill with wine, not the other Netflix and chill) on her evenings. But all three of us manned our little kitchen that fed a lot of the downtown homeless in our corner in Kansas City.

And Dean knew I wasn't known for one to partake in alcoholic libations, but we were here, and I was thirsty.

It was my last day on my medication vacation. I was taking advantage of it.

It was a thing that happened to help cut down on build-up immunity. Sometimes I enjoyed it, but it was usually a whole struggle to get back on and make sure everything was smooth running.

But that wasn't something I was going to think about tonight, though my brain was already starting to go there. Tomorrow I'd go back to living almost like a saint.

Where were my girls with my drinkaloo?

Also, I was firmly not letting myself think of the *he* and that took mundo restraint because he had been a big major part of my daydreams since my junior year in high school through now—especially now since I've been living in the city where he was hockey royalty.

I didn't answer Dean, but spying another Stanley Cup filled with cash, I asked instead, "What's the funding for?"

"Oh!" He perked up, throwing his head back and finishing his drink. A waitress walked by with a tray loaded with fully filled champagne flutes. He snagged two, for himself. "That's why I'm here. I got the final acceptance that the Mustangs are going to dedicate an entire two days to Come Our Way. Two days, Cheyenne. Two days? Can you believe that?" He leaned in, excited, and I could smell how excited he was.

Booze breath. It's a thing.

I edged back a step. "Totally."

So not totally.

"That's awesome."

Really so not awesome.

It was a great PR day for the kitchen and for the team, I was sure that's why they agreed to do it. It wasn't uncommon for Come Our Way to have local celebrities pop in for a day or an hour to volunteer, but the media that followed them was always too much for me. I either stayed in the back kitchen, or I took a personal day. Media days were something *extra* extra. Flashing cameras. Razor-sharp reporters. Sometimes you got a good one who just wanted to spread good news about our mission, but sometimes you got the reporters who wanted to swing things to a more controversial article for the click-baits.

I wasn't down for that poundage.

Plus, the extra buzz in the entire building was like hay fever for my meds. I couldn't handle it, and therapy had taught me to avoid those types of situations, so hence why I usually disappeared—and if the entire team was coming for two days, it'd be insane. I was already not looking forward to it, and yes, I wasn't letting myself think of *him* being in my place of business. At all.

I thought he'd known me in high school, but that turned out to be a result of some slight delusions from my undiagnosed hyper disorder, so that was embarrassing, and then when college rolled around, I intentionally stayed in the background. But if he was going to be at my place for two days—forty-eight hours—there's no way he wouldn't see me, and that information was already bumbling through my head like an intoxicated bee hooked on coke and champagne. It just didn't know what to do or where to sting. Super painful.

Dean was still talking. "...and that's why I'm here. They reciprocated with an invite here, and by the way, it's so on-the-down-low that there's no security outside. Did you see that? To even get in here, you had to know about it."

That made no sense.

Dean didn't care. "And I've already met half the team. Oh!"

His eyes were bouncing around just like my intoxicated inner bee. "I got tickets to their game on Sunday. They rocked preseason, did you see?" He kept edging closer and closer to me the more he talked, something that was so un-Dean-like that I was having a hard time processing all this newness of what was happening around me.

Dean was around the same age as me, a few years older. Coming straight from grad school with a masters in reinvigorating the world to give a fuck about homeless and runaways, he had an axe to grind and an agenda to save the world. He liked to cut loose. You had to in our profession because burnout had the highest success rate, but seeing him this tricked out had that bee flying sideways. He didn't know if he was in my bonnet or my hair braids.

Then I remembered; Dean was a hockey fan.

I was, too, but I kept my undying adoration on the downlow like a lot of things.

Not Dean. He was out of the closet and loud and proud about his love for the Kansas City Mustangs. He also turned traitor and was a Cans fan, as well as the Polars (boo, hiss), but both those teams weren't in this current building or city. So yeah, it made sense now. He was geeking out on the full freakout reader.

That, and I was wondering how much champagne he had already consumed because he just downed both those two flutes in front of me. He was so drunk that my own lit meter was heading down into the empty zone. Not cool. Not cool, indeed, and where were my girls?

Just then, I saw one of them.

And my lit meter skyrocketed right into the red zone.

The crowd parted. I had a clear view right smack to the bar, and there she was. And she wasn't alone.

Sasha had her sultry and seductive pose out, clearly liking what she saw, gazing up at *him*.

Read the rest here!

ALSO BY TIJAN

Rich Prick (standalone) (Blaise and Aspen)

Crew Series (Bren and Cross)

Related books:

Fallen Crest/Roussou Universe

Fallen Crest Series

Crew Series

The Boy I Grew Up With (standalone)

Rich Prick (standalone)

Frisco

Other series:

Broken and Screwed Series (YA/NA)

Jaded Series (YA/NA suspense)

Davy Harwood Series (paranormal)

Carter Reed Series (mafia)

The Insiders

Mafia Standalones:

Cole

Bennett Mafia

Jonah Bennett

Canary

Sports Romance Standalones:

Enemies

Teardrop Shot

Hate To Love You

The Not-Outcast

Hostile

Young Adult Standalones:

Ryan's Bed

A Whole New Crowd

Brady Remington Landed Me in Jail

College Standalones:

Antistepbrother

Kian

Contemporary Romances:

Bad Boy Brody

Home Tears

Fighter

Rockstar Romance Standalone:

Sustain

Paranormal Standalone:

Evil

Micaela's Big Bad

The Tracker

More books to come!

Lightning Source UK Ltd.
Milton Keynes UK
UKHW042247261022
411157UK00004B/271